First German

PART ONE
AT HOME

Kathy Gemmell and Jenny Tyler
Illustrated by Sue Stitt
Designed by Diane Thistlethwaite

D1370194

Consultant: Sandy Walker

CONTENTS
(Part one)

First published in 1993 by Usborne Publishing Ltd.
Usborne House, 83-85 Saffron Hill
London EC1N 8RT, England.
Copyright © 1993 Usborne Publishing Ltd.
First published in America August 1993.
Printed in Portugal.
Universal Edition.

Speaking German

This book is about the Strudel family. They are going to help you learn to speak German.

Word lists
You will find a word list on every double page to tell you what the German words mean.

The little letters are to help you say the German words. Read them as if they were English words.

Hallo
hullaw

Word list

Guten Tag gootn tahg	hello
Hallo hullaw	hi
nein nine	no
ja yah	yes
ich ikh	I
Tschüß tshewss	bye!
du bist dran doo bist dran	your turn

Ich... ikh

Tschüß tshewss

Nein nine

Ja yah

The best way to find out how to say German words is to listen to a German person speaking. Some letters and sounds are a bit different from English. Here are some clues to help you.

When you see a "ch" in German, it is written "kh" in the little letters. Say this like the "h" in "huge". Try saying *ich*, which means "I".

Say "sch" like the "sh" sound in "show".

When you see one of these: ß, just say it like a double "s".

To say the ü, round your lips to say "oo" then say "ee" instead.

The letter "j" in German sounds like the English "y".

Try saying out loud what each person on this page is saying.

See if you can find Josefina the mouse on each double page.

Games with word lists
You can play games with the word lists if you like. Here are some ideas.

1. Cover all the German words and see if you can say the German for each English word. Score a point for each one you can remember.

2. Time yourself and see if you can say the whole list more quickly next time.

3. Race a friend. The first one to say the German for each word scores a point. The winner is the one to score the most points.

4. Play all these games the other way around, saying the English for each German word.

Du bist dran
Look for the *du bist dran* boxes in this book. There is something for you to do in each of them. *Du bist dran* means "your turn".

Look out for the joke bubbles on some of the pages.

3

The Strudels

Here the Strudel family are introducing themselves. *Ich heiße* [ikh hyssa] means "I am called" or "my name is".

Bella has chased Josefina through the Strudel's garden. See if you can follow her route from Onkel Helmut to where she is now. Which members of the family did she pass on the way?

Word list

ich heiße ikh hyssa	I am called
Herr hair	Mr.
Frau fraow	Mrs.
Oma awma	Granny
Onkel onkel	uncle
Tante tanta	aunt
Guten Morgen gootn more gn	good morning
Auf Wiedersehen owf veederzane	goodbye

Names

Strudel shtroodel	Helmut helmoot
Rainer ryner	Max mux
Silvia zilveeya	Bella bella
Markus mahrkoos	Josefina yawzefeena
Uli oolee	Franz frunts
Karin kahrin	Hans hunts
Ilse ilza	Katja katya

Ich heiße Silvia.

Ich heiße Rainer.

Ich heiße Max.

Ich heiße Uli.

Ich heiße Oma Strudel.

Ich heiße Katja.

Ich heiße Markus.

Good morning

Guten Morgen [gootn more gn] means "good morning". Silvia is so sleepy, she has mixed up everyone's names. Say *Guten Morgen* for her, adding the correct name each time.

Guten Morgen Markus

Guten Morgen Oma

Du bist dran
Introduce yourself in German by saying *ich heiße* followed by your name. You can introduce your family and pets, using *er heißt* [air hyste] for males (he is called) and *sie heißt* [zee hyste] for females (she is called).

5

At home

Here is the inside of the Strudel family house. Can you find a way around the house, passing all those who are waiting to tell you the names of the rooms on the way? You must not pass anyone more than once.

Start at the door nearest Frau Strudel and go out by the kitchen door. (Remember that doors are not the only way to get from room to room.)

Bei uns [by oonts] means "at our home". "At my home" is *bei mir* [by meer]. At anyone else's home is *bei* then the name of the person, so "at Silvia's home" would be *bei Silvia* [by zilveeya].

Word list

hier ist *here ist*	here is
das Schlafzimmer *dass shlahf tsimmer*	bedroom
das Badezimmer *dass bahda tsimmer*	bathroom
die Mansarde *dee man sarda*	attic
der Keller *dare keller*	cellar
die Küche *dee kewkha*	kitchen
das Wohnzimmer *dass vawn tsimmer*	lounge
das Eßzimmer *dass ess tsimmer*	dining room
das Haus *dass howss*	house
der Garten *dare gartn*	garden
Mutti *moottee*	mum
bei uns *by oonts*	at our home

Hier ist das Schlafzimmer.

Hier ist das Wohnzimmer.

Hier ist der Garten.

Hier ist Mutti.

Hier ist das Haus.

6

Du bist dran

Take someone around your house and say in German what each room is called using *hier ist* [here ist]. You could also introduce your parents by saying *hier ist Mutti* [here ist moottee] or *hier ist Vati* [here ist fahtee].

Hier ist die Mansarde.

Hier ist das Badezimmer.

Hier ist die Küche.

Hier ist das Eßzimmer.

Hier ist der Keller.

Draw a map

Silvia and Markus have drawn a map of the area near their house and have written all the names in German.

Draw a map of your own area or somewhere you think you would like to live and label it in German.

die Kirche

die Brücke

der Fluß

der Bauernhof

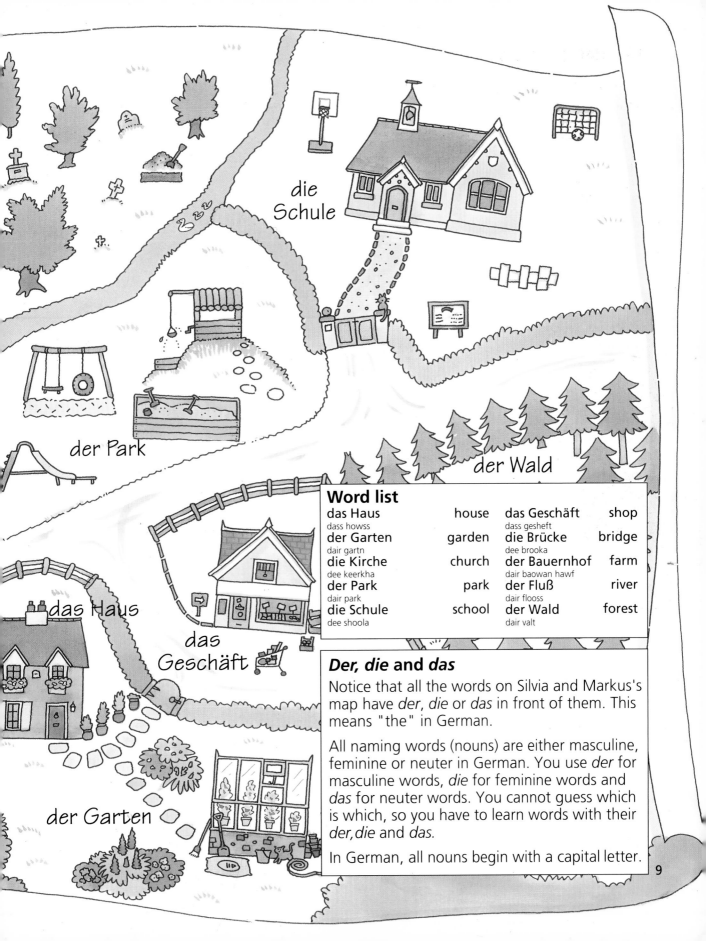

die Schule

der Park

der Wald

das Haus

das Geschäft

der Garten

Word list

das Haus	house	**das Geschäft**	shop
dass howss		dass gesheft	
der Garten	garden	**die Brücke**	bridge
dair gartn		dee brooka	
die Kirche	church	**der Bauernhof**	farm
dee keerkha		dair baowan hawf	
der Park	park	**der Fluß**	river
dair park		dair flooss	
die Schule	school	**der Wald**	forest
dee shoola		dair valt	

Der, die and das

Notice that all the words on Silvia and Markus's map have *der*, *die* or *das* in front of them. This means "the" in German.

All naming words (nouns) are either masculine, feminine or neuter in German. You use *der* for masculine words, *die* for feminine words and *das* for neuter words. You cannot guess which is which, so you have to learn words with their *der, die* and *das*.

In German, all nouns begin with a capital letter.

9

Counting in German

Silvia and Markus stayed up late to finish their map and now can't sleep. In fact, everybody is counting things to help them get to sleep.

Count out loud in German for each person. Who do you think fell asleep first? Use the number list to help you.

Number list

eins ine ts	one
zwei tsvy	two
drei dry	three
vier feer	four
fünf foonf	five
sechs zex	six
sieben zee bn	seven
acht akht	eight
neun noyn	nine
zehn tsain	ten

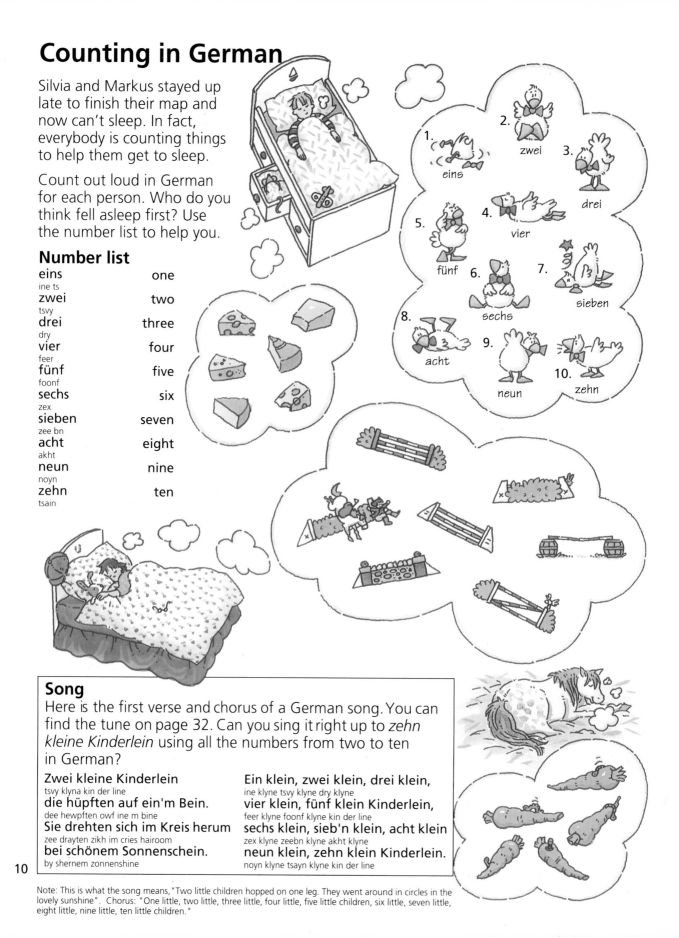

1. eins
2. zwei
3. drei
4. vier
5. fünf
6. sechs
7. sieben
8. acht
9. neun
10. zehn

Song

Here is the first verse and chorus of a German song. You can find the tune on page 32. Can you sing it right up to *zehn kleine Kinderlein* using all the numbers from two to ten in German?

Zwei kleine Kinderlein
tsvy klyna kin der line
die hüpften auf ein'm Bein.
dee hewpften owf ine m bine
Sie drehten sich im Kreis herum
zee drayten zikh im cries hairoom
bei schönem Sonnenschein.
by shernem zonnenshine

Ein klein, zwei klein, drei klein,
ine klyne tsvy klyne dry klyne
vier klein, fünf klein Kinderlein,
feer klyne foonf klyne kin der line
sechs klein, sieb'n klein, acht klein
zex klyne zeebn klyne akht klyne
neun klein, zehn klein Kinderlein.
noyn klyne tsayn klyne kin der line

10

Note: This is what the song means, "Two little children hopped on one leg. They went around in circles in the lovely sunshine". Chorus: "One little, two little, three little, four little, five little children, six little, seven little, eight little, nine little, ten little children."

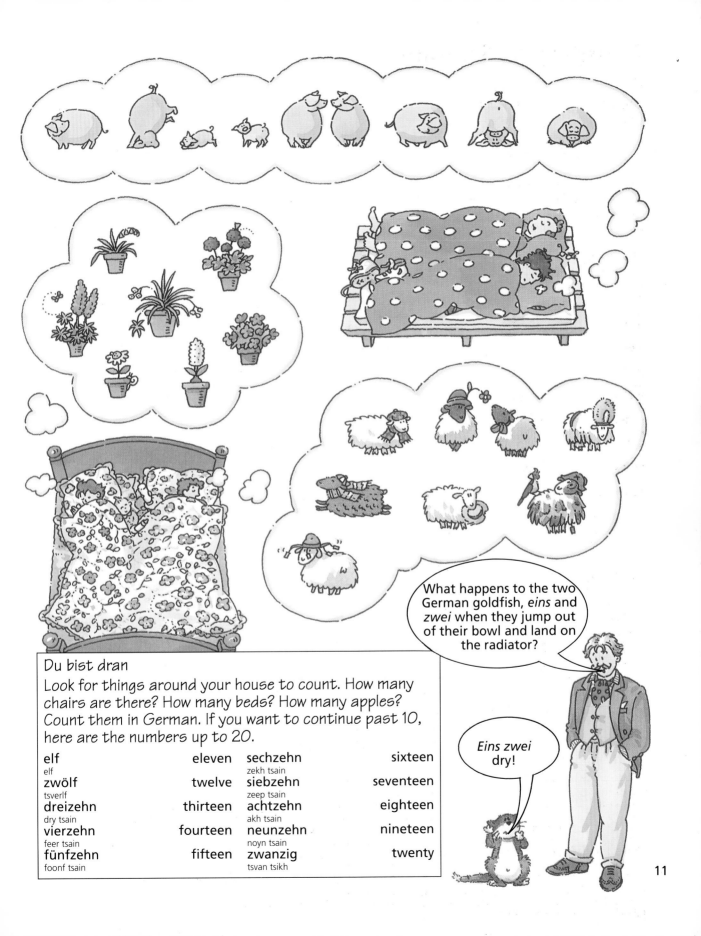

Du bist dran

Look for things around your house to count. How many chairs are there? How many beds? How many apples? Count them in German. If you want to continue past 10, here are the numbers up to 20.

elf elf	eleven	**sechzehn** zekh tsain	sixteen
zwölf tsverlf	twelve	**siebzehn** zeep tsain	seventeen
dreizehn dry tsain	thirteen	**achtzehn** akh tsain	eighteen
vierzehn feer tsain	fourteen	**neunzehn** noyn tsain	nineteen
fünfzehn foonf tsain	fifteen	**zwanzig** tsvan tsikh	twenty

11

Jigsaw puzzles

The next morning everybody is tired and a little bit grumpy. Rainer has brought down some jigsaw puzzles to try and cheer up the family. However, the pieces are all mixed up and Markus is the only one who can see what his puzzle is, *ein Apfel* (an apple).

Can you say in German what all the other puzzles should be? Use the picture list to help you. Only one of the missing pieces cannot be found anywhere. Who will not be able to finish their jigsaw?

Ein, eine and *eins*

In German there are two ways to say "a" something or "one" something, *ein* or *eine*. All *der* and *das* words are *ein* words and all *die* words are *eine* words. To say "one" when you are counting, you say *eins* [ine ts].

Picture list

eine Pflaume ine a pflaow ma **a plum**	**eine Ananas** ine a ananass **a pineapple**	**eine Banane** ine a banana **a banana**	**ein Pfirsich** ine pfeer zikh **a peach**
eine Birne ine a beerna **a pear**	**eine Apfelsine** ine a apfull zeena **an orange**	**ein Apfel** ine ap full **an apple**	

Du bist dran
See if you can remember the words for all these fruits and say what's in your fruit bowl at home.

Answer these questions out loud in German.

Can you see what Josefina is eating? What would Max like to eat?

Song
Here is a song about the fruit and vegetables that Josefina likes and dislikes. Can you guess what any of them are? You can see what all the words mean on page 32.

Kopf‑sa‑lat und Gur‑ke frißt Jo‑se‑fi‑na gern,
kopf za laht oont goor ka frist yaw za fee na gairn

A‑ber Blu‑men‑kohl und Boh‑nen nicht so sehr.
ah ber bloo men kawl oont baw nen nikht zaw zair

Sie mag Pam‑pel‑mu‑se, An‑an‑as und Birn',
zee mahg pum pull moo za an an ass oont beern

A‑ber ih‑re Erb‑sen gibt sie al‑le mir.
ah ber ee ra airb sen geept zee al la meer

13

Joke: What's blue and square? An orange in disguise.

What is it?

Oma has ordered lots of new things for her room. They have just been delivered. *Was ist das?* [vass ist dass] means "what is it?" or "what is that?".

Can you help the rest of the family say in German what is in each parcel? Say *das ist* [dass ist] which means "it is" and then the object. Use the picture list to help you with the names.

Remember that *ein* and *eine* both mean "one" or "a".

Picture list

ein Tisch
ine tish
a table

ein Stuhl
ine shtool
a chair

ein Bett
ine bet
a bed

ein Fernseher
ine fairn zayer
a television

eine Vase
ine a vahza
a vase

ein Wecker
ine vecker
an alarm clock

eine Lampe
ine a lampa
a lamp

eine Tasse
ine a tassa
a cup

ein Teller
ine teller
a plate

Du bist dran

Can you find all the things on the picture list in your own house? If you can, point to each one and say what it is in German, using *das ist* [dass ist] and then the name of the object.

Joke: What's this? It's this the other way around.

15

A day in the life of the Strudels

This is a picture strip of a typical weekend day in the Strudel household - after a good night's sleep this time - but the pictures are all in the wrong order. Can you decide which order they should be in?

Use the word list to help you to say out loud what everyone is saying.

Word list

das Frühstück dass frew shtook	breakfast
das Mittagessen dass mittah gessn	lunch
das Abendessen dass ah bnd essn	dinner
morgens more gns	in the morning
nachmittags nakh mittahks	in the afternoon
Guten Morgen gootn more gn	good morning
Guten Abend gootn ah bnd	good evening
Gute Nacht goota nakht	good night
schlaf gut shlahf goot	sleep well
es ist 3 Uhr ess ist dry oor	it is three o'clock
es ist 8 Uhr ess ist akht oor	it is eight o'clock

Here is a little rhyme about Franz. Can you spot him in two of the pictures?

Das kleine Kaninchen
dass klyna ka neen khn
Steht auf um sieben
shtate owf oom zeebn
Abends um acht
ah bnds oom akht
Sagt "gute Nacht ".
zahkt goota nakht

You can check what all the words mean on page 32.

Guten Appetit [gootn appa teet] is what you say before eating in Germany. It means "enjoy your meal".

Essen kommen [essn kommn] is how you tell people in German to come and eat.

17

Afternoon activity

This afternoon the Strudels are all busy doing things in and around the house. Can you find someone doing each of the things on the word list somewhere in the big picture?

As you find each one, read out loud what that person is saying in German.

Word list

ich esse ikh essa	I am eating
ich lese ikh layza	I am reading
ich laufe ikh laowfa	I am running
ich gehe ikh gaya	I am walking
ich singe ikh zinga	I am singing
ich trinke ikh trinka	I am drinking
ich spreche ikh shprekha	I am speaking
ich schlafe ikh shlahfa	I am sleeping
ich arbeite ikh ahr byta	I am working
ich schwimme ikh shvimma	I am swimming
ich falle ikh falla	I am falling
ich gehe aus ikh gaya owss	I am going out
ich springe ikh shpringa	I am jumping

Du bist dran
Was machst du?
[vass makhst doo].
What are you doing at the moment? You're probably reading, so you say *ich lese* [ich layza]. See if you can do all the other things in the picture and remember how to say them in German.

18

Joke: What has eight legs and spins? A spider in a washing machine.

19

Happy birthday

The next day is Oma's birthday and the family is having a party for her. There are lots of different kinds of food because everyone likes different things.

To say you like something in German you say *ich mag* [ikh mahg] and then the thing you like. To say you don't like something you say the thing you don't like and then *mag ich nicht* [mahg ikh nikht].

"Happy birthday" in German is *Herzlichen Glückwunsch zum Geburtstag* [hairtslikhn glookvoontsh tsoom gaboorts tahg].

Word list

ich mag _(ikh mahg)_	I like
...mag ich nicht _(mahg ikh nikht)_	I don't like...
Obst _(awpst)_	fruit
Käse _(kayza)_	cheese
Brot _(brawt)_	bread
Gemüse _(gamooza)_	vegetables
Marmelade _(marmalahda)_	jam
Pralinen _(prah leenan)_	chocolates
Salat _(zallaht)_	salad
Schinken _(shinkan)_	ham
Suppe _(zooppa)_	soup
Pommes frites _(pom frit)_	french fries
Torten _(tortn)_	cakes
Würstchen _(verst khen)_	sausages

Ich mag Schinken.

Herzlichen Glückwunsch zum Geburtstag.

Ich mag Brot.

Ich mag Marmelade.

Ich mag Pralinen.

Can you see which people do not like the food in front of them? Say out loud in German what they are thinking.

What do you think Silvia is saying? How would Max say what he likes in German?

In German most cakes are called *Torten* but some sponge cakes are called *Kuchen* [kookhen].

21

Silvia goes shopping

Today is a school holiday and Silvia has gone to do the shopping.

Can you see from the picture what Silvia is asking for? *Ich möchte* [ikh merkhte] means "I would like" and *und* [oont] means "and".

Now try to ask for all the items on Silvia's shopping list in German. Remember to say "please", *bitte* [bitta] and "thank you", *danke schön* [dunka shern].

Der, *die* and *das* all change to *die* when you are talking about more than one thing. The name of the thing usually changes a bit as well.

Ich möchte eine Zeitung und ein Eis, bitte.

Liste
4 Äpfel
9 Bananen
8 Brötchen
5 Zwiebeln
6 Fische
2 Torten

Can you see from the picture how to say "How much does that come to?" in German? Say it out loud.

What do you think Uli will ask for? Say it for him.

Number reminder

eins	one	sechs	six
ine ts		zex	
zwei	two	sieben	seven
tsvy		zee bn	
drei	three	acht	eight
dry		akht	
vier	four	neun	nine
feer		noyn	
fünf	five	zehn	ten
foonf		tsain	

Du bist dran
Wieviel [vee feel] means "how much" in German and *wieviele* [vee feela] means "how many". Can you answer the following questions by looking at the picture? Use the number reminder to help you count up in German how many there are.

Wieviele Blumen?
Wieviele Hüte?
Wieviele Katzen?

Note: The money used in Germany is German Marks, called *Deutschmark* (DM), and *Pfennigs* (Pf). There are 100 Pfennigs to a Mark.

Word list

ich möchte *ikh merkhte*	I would like
die Katze *dee katsa*	cat
der Apfel *dair apfull*	apple
die Banane *dee banana*	banana
das Brötchen *dass brert khen*	roll
die Zwiebel *dee tsveebel*	onion
das macht...Mark *dass makht...mark*	that's...Mark
wieviel macht das? *vee feel makht dass*	how much does that come to?
der Fisch *dair fish*	fish
die Blume *dee blooma*	flower
die Torte *dee torta*	cake
das Eis *dass ice*	ice cream cone
bitte *bitta*	please
danke schön *dunka shern*	thank you
der Hut *dair hoot*	hat
die Zeitung *dee tsy toong*	newspaper

Joke: Which dogs don't bite? Hot dogs.

23

Market day

Later on, the whole family goes down to the market. Everybody in the village seems to be there. It is so crowded that the Strudels have split up and are all doing things in different parts of the market.

Uli asks where Franz is and the butcher points to him. *Wo ist* [vaw ist] means "where is" and *da ist Franz* [dah ist frunts] means "there's Franz".

Can you spot all of the Strudels in the crowd? Point to each one and say *da ist* [dah ist] followed by the person's name.

Wo ist Bella?

Wo ist Max?

Wo ist Josefina?

Wo ist Franz?

Da ist Franz.

Danke schön

Wo gehst
vaw gayst
du hin?
doo hin

Ich ziehe um.
ikh tseeya oom

24

Joke: Where are you going? I'm moving (house).

Dominoes to make

For something to do at home, Silvia and Markus have invented a game of dominoes which uses German colours. Here's how to make one like theirs and play it.

1. Cut your cardboard into 28 rectangles about 8cm long and 4cm wide (3in by 1½in). You can make the rectangles bigger if you have more cardboard.

You will need:
white cardboard (at least 32cm by 28 cm, 13in by 11in), felt tips, scissors and a black pen.

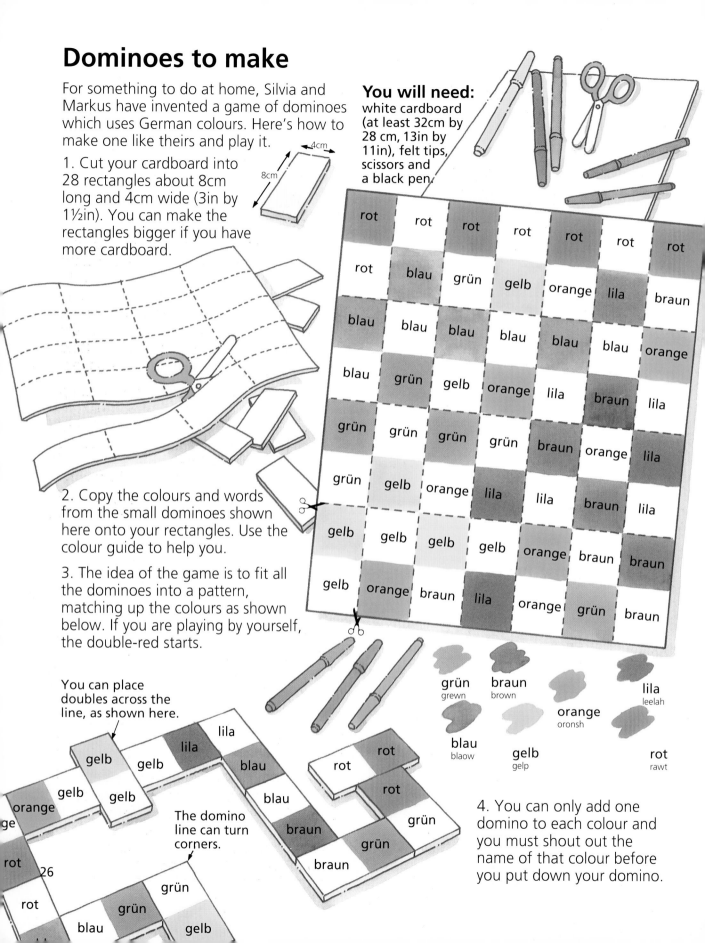

8cm

4cm

2. Copy the colours and words from the small dominoes shown here onto your rectangles. Use the colour guide to help you.

3. The idea of the game is to fit all the dominoes into a pattern, matching up the colours as shown below. If you are playing by yourself, the double-red starts.

You can place doubles across the line, as shown here.

The domino line can turn corners.

rot	rot	rot	rot	rot	rot	rot
rot	blau	grün	gelb	orange	lila	braun
blau	blau	blau	blau	blau	blau	orange
blau	grün	gelb	orange	lila	braun	lila
grün	grün	grün	grün	braun	orange	lila
grün	gelb	orange	lila	lila	braun	lila
gelb	gelb	gelb	gelb	orange	braun	braun
gelb	orange	braun	lila	orange	grün	braun

grün grewn **braun** brown **lila** leelah

orange oronsh

blau blaow **gelb** gelp **rot** rawt

4. You can only add one domino to each colour and you must shout out the name of that colour before you put down your domino.

26

5. If you are playing with a friend, first spread the dominoes out, face-down, on the table or floor. Take seven dominoes each and put them face-up in front of you. These form your "hand".

6. The idea of this game is to get rid of all the dominoes in your hand and the first person to do so is the winner.

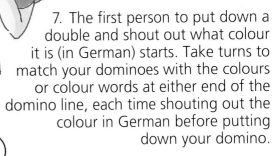

Du bist dran.

7. The first person to put down a double and shout out what colour it is (in German) starts. Take turns to match your dominoes with the colours or colour words at either end of the domino line, each time shouting out the colour in German before putting down your domino.

8. If you can't go, you must pick up a spare domino if there is one left, or miss a turn if there is not.

Word list

du bist dran	your turn
doo bist dran	
ich habe gewonnen	I've won
ikh hahba gavonnen	

Ich habe gewonnen.

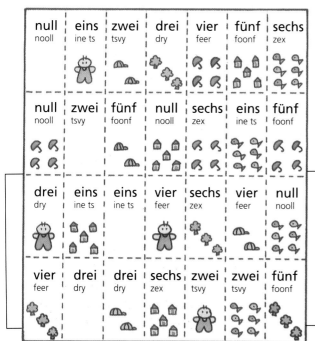

null	eins	zwei	drei	vier	fünf	sechs
nooll	ine ts	tsvy	dry	feer	foonf	zex

null	zwei	fünf	null	sechs	eins	fünf
nooll	tsvy	foonf	nooll	zex	ine ts	foonf

drei	eins	eins	vier	sechs	vier	null
dry	ine ts	ine ts	feer	zex	feer	nooll

vier	drei	drei	sechs	zwei	zwei	fünf
feer	dry	dry	zex	tsvy	tsvy	foonf

Number dominoes

You could also make German number dominoes. Copy these dominoes onto pieces of cardboard (the same as the ones used for Colour dominoes) and play in the same way, this time matching up the number of objects with the number in German. The double-six fish starts.

27

Memory game

Here is a game which you can play again and again. The idea is to get to the finish as quickly as possible.

You will need:
a dice
a clock or watch

How to play

Look at the time when you start. Throw the dice and count with your finger the number of squares shown on the dice. Say the answer to the question on that square out loud then shake again.

If you land on a square with no question on it, shake again and move on.

All the answers can be found in this part of the book, so if you can't remember or are not sure, look back through the book until you find the correct answer.

Look at the time again when you finish. Can you do it more quickly next time?

Which way would you say *die Kirche*?

1. dye keerkha
2. dee keerkha
3. dee kersha

Tell Markus how to ask for an ice cream cone in German.

Wieviele Blumen?

Say "yes" in German.

What would Markus say if you asked, *Was machst du?*

Say "hi" in German.

Was ist das?

How do you introduce yourself in German?

1. rot
2. lila
3. gelb

Say "hello" in German.

Which of these describes Katja's balloon?

What is Silvia saying to Herr Grün?

Say "good night" in German.

Which of these is Silvia saying?

Say "I am eating" in German.

How will Markus tell his friend what Josefina's name is?

1. Ich mag Käse
2. Ich mag Schinken
3. Ich mag Pralinen

Start
shtart
(start)

28

What comes after achtzehn?

Was ist das?

Was ist das?

How do you say "the garden" in German?

Which of these numbers is in the wrong place?

1 5
4
2 3

eins
zwei
fünf
drei
vier

How would you ask for two apples in German?

How would you say "a peach" in German?

1. een far zish
2. ine peer zik
3. ine pfeer zikh

Say the missing word, das ist eine...

How do you say "at my home" in German?

Was ist das?

Say "thank you" in German.

20

How do you say "twenty" in German?

Which room do you think Max is in? Say it in German.

Was ist das?

What happens to the two German goldfish, eins and zwei when they jump out of their bowl onto the radiator?

What comes after sieben?

15

How do you say "fifteen" in German?

How will Silvia say what she is doing in German?

Was ist das?

What do you say in Germany before starting a meal?

Was ist das?

Say "good-bye" in German.

How do you say "how much is it?" in German?

Wieviele Äpfel?

How would you say ich heiße?

What would Uli say if you asked, Was machst du, Uli?

1. ik hyba
2. ikh hyssa
3. ish heesa

Ziel
tseel
(end)

Word list (part one)

Here is a list of all the German words and phrases used in this part of the book in alphabetical order. You can use the list either to check quickly what a word means, or to test yourself. Cover up any German or English word or phrase and see if you can say its translation. (Remember that some words change slightly when you are talking about more than one thing.)

Abendessen (das)	ah bnd essn	*dinner*
abends	ah bnds	*in the evening*
aber	ah ber	*but*
acht	akht	*eight*
achtzehn	akh tsain	*eighteen*
Ananas (die)	ananass	*pineapple*
Apfel (der)	ap full	*apple*
Äpfel (die)	ep full	*apples*
Apfelsine (die)	ap full zeena	*orange*
Auf Wiedersehen	owf veederzane	*goodbye*
Badezimmer (das)	bahda tsimmer	*bathroom*
Banane (die)	banana	*banana*
Bauernhof (der)	baowan hawf	*farm*
bei mir	by meer	*at my home*
Bein (das)	bine	*leg*
Bett (das)	bet	*bed*
Birne (die)	beerna	*pear*
bitte	bitta	*please*
blau	blaow	*blue*
Blume (die)	blooma	*flower*
Blumenkohl (der)	bloo men kawl	*cauliflower*
Bohnen (die)	baw nen	*beans*
braun	brown	*brown*
Brot (das)	brawt	*bread*
Brötchen (das)	brert khen	*roll*
Brücke (die)	brooka*	*bridge*
da ist (Franz)	dah ist (frunts)	*there's (Franz)*
danke schön	dunka shern	*thank you very much*
das ist	dass ist	*it/that is*
das macht...Mark	dass makht..mark	*that makes...Marks*
der, die, das	dair, dee, dass	*the*
drei	dry	*three*
dreizehn	dry tsain	*thirteen*
du bist dran	doo bist dran	*your turn*
ein, eine	ine, ine a	*a/an/one*
eins	ine ts	*one*
Eis (das)	ice	*ice cream cone*
elf	elf	*eleven*
er	air	*he*
er dreht sich	air drayt zikh	*he spins*
er heißt	air hyste	*he is called*

er sagt	air zahkt	*he says*
er steht auf	air shtate owf	*he gets up*
Erbsen (die)	airb sen	*peas*
es	ess	*it*
es ist ...Uhr	ess ist...oor	*it is...o'clock*
essen kommen	essn kommn	*come and eat*
Eßzimmer (das)	ess tsimmer	*dining room*
Fernseher (der)	fairn zayer	*television*
Fisch (der)	fish	*fish*
Fluß (der)	flooss*	*river*
Frau	fraow	*Mrs.*
Frühstück (das)	frew shtook*	*breakfast*
fünf	foonf*	*five*
fünfzehn	foonf tsain*	*fifteen*
Garten (der)	gartn	*garden*
gelb	gelp	*yellow*
Gemüse (das)	gamooza	*vegetables*
Geschäft (das)	gesheft	*shop*
grün	grewn	*green*
Gurke (die)	goorka	*cucumber*
Guten Abend	gootn ah bnd	*good evening*
Guten Appetit	gootn appateet	*enjoy your meal*
Guten Morgen	gootn more gn	*good morning*
Gute Nacht	goota nakht	*good night*
Guten Tag	gootn tahg	*hello*
Hallo	hullaw	*hi*
Haus (das)	howss	*house*
Herr	hair	*Mr.*
Herzlichen Glückwunsch zum Geburtstag	hairtslikhn glookvoontsh* tsoom* gaboorts tahg	*happy birthday*
hier ist	here ist	*here is*
Hund (der)	hoont*	*dog*
Hut (der)	hoot	*hat*
ich	ikh	*I*
ich arbeite	ikh ahr byta	*I am working*
ich esse	ikh essa	*I am eating*
ich falle	ikh falla	*I am falling*
ich gehe	ikh gaya	*I am walking*
ich gehe aus	ikh gaya owss	*I am going out*
ich habe gewonnen	ikh hahba gavonnen	*I've won*
ich heiße	ikh hyssa	*I am called*
ich laufe	ikh laowfa	*I am running*
ich lese	ikh layza	*I am reading*
ich mag	ikh mahg	*I like*
ich möchte	ikh merkhta	*I would like*
ich schlafe	ikh shlahfa	*I am sleeping*
ich schwimme	ikh shvimma	*I am swimming*
ich singe	ikh zinga	*I am singing*

30

*The 'oo' sound in these words is like the 'u' in 'put'.

ich spreche	ikh shprekha	*I am speaking*
ich springe	ikh shpringa	*I am jumping*
ich trinke	ikh trinka	*I am drinking*
ich ziehe um	ikh tseeya oom*	*I am moving (house)*
im Kreis	im cries	*in a circle*
ja	yah	*yes*
Kaninchen (das)	ka neen khn	*rabbit*
Käse (der)	kayza	*cheese*
Katze (die)	katsa	*cat*
Keller (der)	keller	*cellar*
Kirche (die)	keerkha	*church*
kleine	klyna	*little*
Kopfsalat (der)	kopf za laht	*lettuce*
Küche (die)	kewkha	*kitchen*
Lampe (die)	lampa	*lamp*
lila	leelah	*purple*
Liste (die)	lissta	*list*
mag ich nicht	mahg ikh nikht	*I don't like*
Mansarde (die)	man sarda	*attic*
Marmelade (die)	marmalahda	*jam*
Mittagessen (das)	mittah gessn	*lunch*
morgens	more gns	*in the morning*
Mutti	moottee*	*mum*
nachmittags	nakh mittahks	*in the afternoon*
nein	nine	*no*
neun	noyn	*nine*
neunzehn	noyn tsain	*nineteen*
null	nooll*	*zero*
Obst (das)	awpst	*fruit*
Oma (die)	awma	*grandma*
Onkel (der)	onkel	*uncle*
orange	oronsh	*orange*
Pampelmuse (die)	pum pull mooza	*grapefruit*
Park (der)	park	*park*
Pfirsich (der)	pfeer zikh	*peach*
Pflaume (die)	pflaow ma	*plum*
Pralinen (die)	prah leenan	*chocolates*
Pommes frites (die)	pom frit	*french fries*
rot	rawt	*red*
Salat (der)	zallaht	*salad*
schlaf gut	shlahf goot	*sleep well*
Schlafzimmer (das)	shlahf tsimmer	*bedroom*
Schinken (der)	shinkan	*ham*
Schule (die)	shoola	*school*
sechs	zex	*six*
sechzehn	zekh tsain	*sixteen*
sie	zee	*she*
sieben	zeebn	*seven*
siebzehn	zeep tsain	*seventeen*
sie heißt	zee hyste	*she is called*
Spinne (die)	shpinna	*spider*
Start	shtart	*start*
Stuhl (der)	shtool	*chair*
Suppe (die)	zooppa*	*soup*
Tante (die)	tanta	*aunt*
Tasse (die)	tassa	*cup*
Teller (der)	teller	*plate*
Tisch (der)	tish	*table*
Torte (die)	torta	*cake*
Tschüß	tshewss	*bye*
um	oom*	*at*
umgekehrt	oom gekairt*	*the other way around*
und	oont*	*and*
Vase (die)	vahza	*vase*
Vati	fahtee	*dad*
verkleidete	fairklydet a	*in disguise*
vier	feer	*four*
viereckig	feer eckig	*square*
vierzehn	feer tsain	*fourteen*
Wald (der)	valt	*wood*
was ist das?	vass ist dass	*what is it/that?*
was machst du?	vass makhst doo	*what are you doing?*
was magst du?	vass mahgst doo	*what do you like?*
was magst du nicht?	vass mahgst doo nicht	*what do you not like?*
Waschmaschine (die)	vashma sheena	*washing machine*
Wecker (der)	vecker	*alarm clock*
welche..?	vellkha	*which..?*
wieviele?	vee feela	*how many?*
wieviel macht das?	vee feel makht dass	*how much does that come to?*
wo gehst du hin?	vaw gayst doo hin	*where are you going?*
Wohnzimmer (das)	vawn tsimmer	*living room*
wo ist..?	vaw ist	*where is..?*
Würstchen (das)	verst khen	*sausage*
zehn	tsain	*ten*
Zeitung (die)	tsy toong*	*newspaper*
Ziel	tseel	*end*
zwanzig	tsvan tsikh	*twenty*
zwei	tsvy	*two*
Zwiebel (die)	tsveebel	*onion*
zwölf	tsverlf	*twelve*

Answers (part one)

PAGE 4-5

Bella passed *Onkel Helmut, Herr Strudel, Franz, Tante Ilse, Uli, Rainer, Silvia, Max, Katja, Markus, Oma* and *Frau Strudel.*

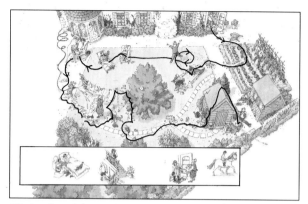

Silvia should say *Guten Morgen Bella, Guten Morgen Markus* and *Guten Morgen Oma.*

PAGE 6-7

This is the way you must go:

PAGE 10-11

Max fell asleep first - he only counted to five before falling asleep. The tune for the song is:

Zwei klei-ne Kin-der-lein die hüpf-ten auf ein'm Bein. Sie
tsvy   kly na kin der line dee hewpf ten owf ine m bine   zee

dreh-ten sich im Kreis her-um bei schö-nem Sonn-en - schein.
dray ten zikh im cries hair oom by sher nem zonn en   shine

Refrain

Ein klein, zwei klein, drei klein, vier klein, fünf klein Kin-der - lein,
ine klyne tsvy klyne dry klyne feer klyne foonf klyne kin der line

Sechs klein, sieb'n klein, acht klein, neun klein, zehn klein Kin-der - lein.
zex klyne zeebn klyne akht klyne noyn klyne tsayn klyne kin der line

PAGE 12-13

What everyone's jigsaws were:
Herr Strudel-*ein Pfirsich* (a peach),
Tante Ilse-*eine Birne* (a pear),
Karin-*eine Banane* (a banana),
Katja-*eine Ananas* (a pineapple),
Uli-*eine Pflaume* (a plum),
Silvia-*eine Apfelsine* (an orange).

Herr Strudel will not be able to finish his jigsaw.

The answers to the questions are:
Josefina - *eine Pflaume* (a plum),
Max - *ein Apfel* (an apple).

Here is what the words of the song mean in English:
Josefina likes eating
Lettuce and cucumber,
But she doesn't like
Cauliflower and beans much.
She likes grapefruit,
Pineapple and pear,
But all her peas,
She gives to me.

PAGE 16-17

The right order for the pictures is: D F G H B E C A

Here is the rhyme in English:
The little rabbit
Gets up at seven,
In the evening at eight
(He) says "goodnight".

PAGE 20-21

Markus is thinking *Käse mag ich nicht.*
Rainer is thing *Suppe mag ich nicht.*
Onkel Helmut is thinking *Würstchen mag ich nicht.*
Silvia is saying *Ich mag Pommes frites.*
Max would say *Ich mag Obst.*

PAGE 22-23

Silvia is asking for a newspaper and an ice cream cone.

"How much is it?" is *wieviel macht das?*
Uli is going to say *Ich möchte ein Eis, bitte.*
There are:
9 *Blumen*
5 *Hüte*
6 *Katzen*

First German

PART 2: ON HOLIDAY

Kathy Gemmell and Jenny Tyler
Illustrated by Sue Stitt
Designed by Diane Thistlethwaite

Consultant: Sandy Walker

CONTENTS
(part 2)

In this part of the book the Strudels are at the beach for a week. They are going to help you to learn more German.

Remember that you will find a word list on every double page to tell you what the German words mean.

Hallo
hullaw

Don't forget that the little letters are to help you say the German words.

Ich heiße
ikh hyssa
Rainer.
ryner

Er heißt
air hyste
Rainer.
ryner

Ich spreche
ikh shprekha
Deutsch.
doytsh

Guten Abend
gootn ah bnd

Guten Tag
gootn tahg

Word list

Guten Tag gootn tahg	hello
Hallo hullaw	hi
ich heiße ikh hyssa	I am called
er heißt air hyste	he is called
ich spreche	I speak
Deutsch ikh shprekha doytsh	German
das Spiel dass shpeel	the game
Guten Abend gootn ah bnd	good evening

Try to listen to real German people speaking whenever you can. Here are some more clues to help you say some of the sounds which are different from English.

When you see "ie" in German, say it like "ee" in English. Try saying *das Spiel* [dass shpeel] which means "the game".

Remember that when you see one of these: ß, say it like a double "s".

Also remember that you say the German "ch" like the "h" in "huge", but "sch" like the "sh" in "show". Say out loud that you speak German: *Ich spreche Deutsch* [ikh shprekha doytsh].

Say the letter "u" in German like the "u" in "rule".

Try saying out loud what each person on this page is saying.

Remember to look for Josefina the mouse on each double page.

Spiele - games

Remember that you can play games with the word lists. Trying to remember the German for each English word is a good way to learn.

Did you notice that "games", *die Spiele* [dee shpeela], is different from the word for "game" on the word list? Most German words change when you are talking about more than one thing (plural).

Can you spot how each of these words change?

der Vogel (bird)	*die Vögel*
der Ball (ball)	*die Bälle*
die Katze (cat)	*die Katzen*
das Mädchen(girl)	*die Mädchen*
das Ohr (ear)	*die Ohren*
das Nest (nest)	*die Nester*
das Auto (car)	*die Autos*
das Bein (leg)	*die Beine*
das Handtuch (towel)	*die Handtücher*

You can check on page 64.

Du bist dran
Don't forget that *du bist dran* means "your turn". Remember to look for the *du bist dran* boxes in this part of the book.

Remember to look out for the joke bubbles on some of the pages.

35

Setting off

The Strudel family are getting ready to go away to the beach for a week. Unfortunately, everyone seems to have lost something.

Can you help by answering all of their questions? *Wo ist* [vaw ist] means "where is" Use the word list to know what the other words mean.

Everything can be found somewhere in the picture. Point to each missing object and say "it's there" in German. This is *da ist er* [dah ist air] if the object has *der* before it, or *da ist sie* [dah ist zee] if the object has *die* before it. Say *da ist es* [dah ist ess] if the object has *das* before it.

Word list

wo ist	vaw ist	where is
da ist er	dah ist air	he/it is there
da ist sie	dah ist zee	she/it is there
da ist es	dah ist ess	it is there
der Ball	dair bal	ball
die Zeitung	dee tsy toong	newspaper
die Angelrute	dee ang el roota	fishing rod
der Korb	dair korp	basket
der Regenschirm	dair ray gun sheerm	umbrella
das Radio	dass rah dee aw	radio
das Handtuch	dass rah dee aw	towel
das Auto	dass owtaw	car
Herr	hair	Mr.
Oma	awma	Granny

Names

Strudel	Silvia	Katja
shtroodel	zilveeya	katya

Der, die and das

Remember that *der, die* and *das* all mean "the". In German, all naming words (nouns) are either masculine, feminine or neuter. Masculine words have *der* before them, feminine words have *die* before them and neuter words have *das* before them.

Don't forget to learn words with their *der, die* or *das*.

37

Joke: What's yellow and black and wears a straw hat? A bee on holiday.

On the road

The Strudels quickly get lost. They've also lost some of their luggage on the way. Can you find it for them by following their route so far? Start at their house, which is *bei den Strudels* [by dane shtroodels] in German.

Now they want to see all the places on the word list on their way to the beach. Which way should they go? They can only pass each place once.

Word list

Remember, *der, die* and *das* all mean "the".

das Häuschen das hoyss khen	cottage
der Campingplatz dair kemping pluts	campsite
die Burg dee boorg	castle
das Café dass ka fay	café
der Bahnhof dair bahn hawf	station
der See dair zay	lake
der Wald dair valt	forest
der Bauernhof dair baowan hawf	farm
das blaue Haus dass blaowa howss	blue house
der Markt dair markt	market
der Strand dair shtrunt	beach

Can you find the windmill, the field, the church and the school on the map? Point to them and say their names out loud in German.

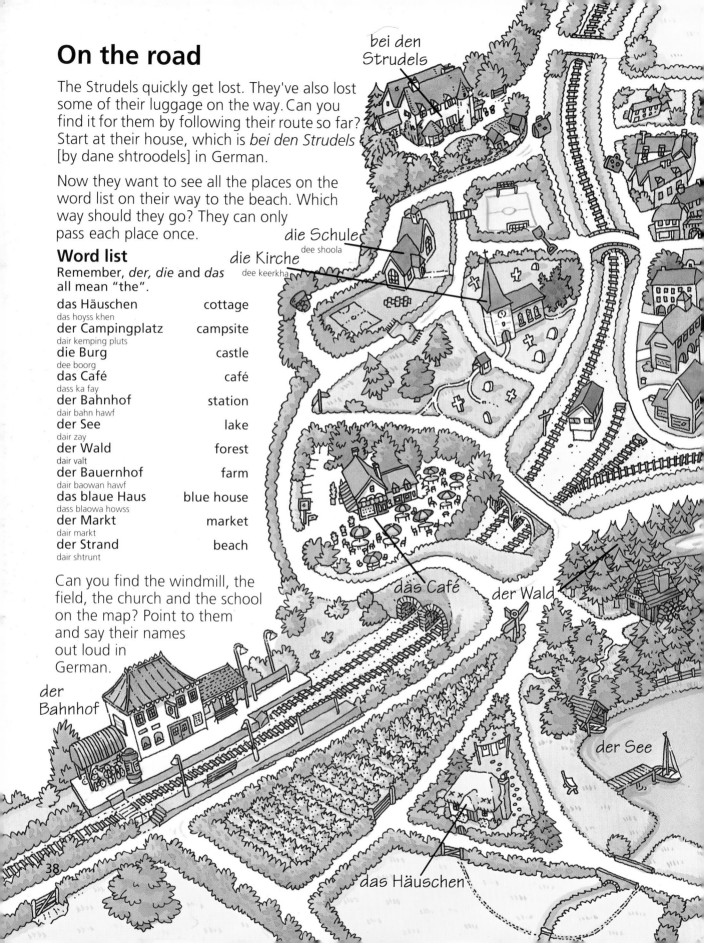

bei den Strudels

die Schule
dee shoola

die Kirche
dee keerkha

däs Café

der Wald

der Bahnhof

der See

das Häuschen

38

der Markt

der Strand

die Windmühle
dee vintmoola

die Burg

das blaue Haus

der Bauernhof
das Feld
dass felt

Du bist dran
Imagine you're going away for a week. Draw a map showing where you are going and label all the places you will pass in German.

der Campingplatz

39

Counting game

Silvia, Markus, Katja and Uli set off to explore the countryside around the chalet where they are staying. In the forest they play a game to see who can spot the most wildlife. They write down how many of each thing they see.

Only one person has counted everything correctly. Can you see from their lists and the picture who it is?

Use the number key and word list to help you with the words.

Number key

eins ine ts	one	sechs zex	six
zwei tsvy	two	sieben zeebn	seven
drei dry	three	acht akht	eight
vier feer	four	neun noyn	nine
fünf foonf	five	zehn tsayn	ten

Names

Markus mahrkoos	Uli oolee

How many?

To ask "How many...are there?" in German, you say *Wieviele ... gibt es?* [vee feela gipt es]. To answer, you say *Es gibt* [ess gipt] and then the number of things. So to answer *Wieviele Katzen gibt es?* [vee feela katsn gipt ess] you would say *Es gibt zwei Katzen* [ess gipt tsvy katsn]. Can you answer the following questions in German?

Wieviele Bäume gibt es?

Wieviele Nester gibt es?

Wieviele Blumen gibt es?

Word list

Most naming words (nouns) change in the plural (when there is more than one) in German. *Der, die* and *das* are *die* in the plural.

die Kaninchen dee ka neen khen	rabbits
eine Maus ine a mouse	a mouse
die Mäuse dee moyza	mice
eine Katze, die Katzen ine a katsa, dee katsn	a cat, cats
die Hirsche dee heersha	stags
die Vögel dee fergl	birds
die Schlangen dee shlungn	snakes
die Füchse dee fooksa	foxes
die Schmetterlinge dee shmetterlinga	butterflies
die Bäume dee boyma	trees
die Blumen dee bloomn	flowers
ein Nest, die Nester ine nest, dee nester	a nest, nests
wieviele vee feela	how many
es gibt ess gipt	there is/are

Markus
sieben Vögel
acht Kaninchen
eine Maus
sechs Hirsche
vier Füchse
zwei Katzen
fünf Schmetterlinge
drei Schlangen

Katja
acht Vögel
sieben Kaninchen
zwei Mäuse
drei Hirsche
fünf Füchse
eine Katze
zehn Schmetterlinge
zwei Schlangen

Uli
acht Vögel
acht Kaninchen
eine Maus
drei Hirsche
vier Füchse
eine Katze
neun Schmetterlinge
zwei Schlangen

Silvia
acht Vögel
acht Kaninchen
drei Mäuse
vier Hirsche
vier Füchse
eine Katze
sieben Schmetterlinge
zwei Schlangen

*Joke: What's the difference between a Siberian tiger and a Bengal tiger? 10 000km. (In Germany, distance is measured in km, not miles. To change miles to km, multiply by 8 and divide by 5.)

On the beach

On the first day at the beach, the Strudel children join a beach club. To help everyone get to know each other, they have all made name and age badges to wear.

Wie alt bist du? [vee ult bist doo] means "How old are you?" Katja answers, *Ich bin sieben Jahre alt* [ikh bin zeebn yahra ult], which means "I am seven years old".

Can you say in German what Uli, Markus and Silvia are saying? What would either of the twins say? Use the number list to help you.

Number list

eins*	one	sechs	six
ine ts		zex	
zwei	two	sieben	seven
tsvy		zeebn	
drei	three	acht	eight
dry		akht	
vier	four	neun	nine
feer		noyn	
fünf	five	zehn	ten
foonf		tsayn	

*Eins only means "one" when you are counting.
"One year old" is ein Jahr alt [ine yahr ult].

Word list

wie alt bist du?	how old are you?
vee ult bist doo	
ich bin...Jahre alt	I'm...years old
ikh bin...yahra ult	
wie heißt du?	what are you called?
vee hyste doo	
ich heiße	I am called, my name is
ikh hyssa	

Wie alt bist du?

Markus Ich bin 8 Jahre alt.

Ich bin 1 Jahr alt.

Du bist dran

Make your own name and age badge in German. You will need: a piece of cardboard, a safety pin, sticky tape, a pen or pencil, scissors and a cup or mug.

1. Draw a circle on the piece of cardboard, using the bottom of a cup (or any round object of the size you want your badge to be) to draw a perfect circle. Then cut it out.

2. Wie heißt du? [vee hyste doo]. Write on the circle what you are called and how old you are in German. Ich heiße [ikh hyssa] means "I am called".

Look at the picture to see how to write how old you are.

Ich heiße Markus.
Ich bin 8 Jahre alt.

3. Stick a pin to the back of the circle with sticky tape. (Remember to only stick down one side of the pin so that it can still open).

43

Treasure hunt

Klaus [klowss], the leader of the beach club, has organized a treasure hunt. He has hidden the treasure in one of the red boxes in the picture.

Using the word and picture lists to help you, can you follow the clues below to find out which of the red boxes holds the treasure?

As you say each clue out loud in German, point to any of the red boxes you can see in that place. The treasure box is the only one which is in all the places on the list of clues.

Hinweise (Clues)
Auf dem Campingplatz
Hinter dem Zelt
Vor dem Baum
Neben dem Tor
Auf der Mauer
Unter dem Eimer

Word list

der Campingplatz	campsite
dair kemping pluts	
das Tor	gate
dass tawr	
der Baum	tree
dair baowm	
das Zelt	tent
dass tsellt	
die Mauer	wall
dee maower	
der Eimer	bucket
dair eyemer	

Picture list

hinter
hinter

auf
owf

unter
oonter

vor
fore

in
in

neben
naybn

Du bist dran

You could make up your own treasure hunt using German clues. Hide something and write down how to find it in German using Klaus's clues and/or any of the phrases below.

hinter dem Vorhang
hinter dame forehung

unter dem Tisch
oonter dame tish

vor dem Sofa
fore dame zawfah

unter dem Bett
oonter dame bet

auf dem Stein
owf dame shtyne

in dem Wäschekorb
in dame veshakorp

vor dem Spiegel
fore dame shpeegl

neben der Pflanze
naybn dair pfluntsa

hinter dem Papierkorb
hinter dame pupeerkorp

in dem Schrank
in dame shrunk

neben dem Fernseher
naybn dame fairn zayer

45

Guess who?

Klaus's next activity for the beach club is the Guess who? game. Everyone must pretend to be someone or something else. Klaus must guess what each child is pretending to be.

Can you see who is a mouse? Who is a king? *Ich bin* [ikh bin] means "I am". Using the word list to help you, say out loud in German what each child is thinking.

Word list

ich bin ikh bin	I am	**ein Mädchen** ein mate khen	a girl
du bist doo bist	you are	**ein Junge** ein yoonga	a boy
ja yah	yes	**ein Mann** ine mun	a man
nein nine	no	**ein Vogel** ine fawgl	a bird
eine Katze ine a katza	a cat	**eine Königin** ine a kernig in	a queen
ein Pferd ine pfairt	a horse	**ein König** ine kernikh	a king
ein Hund ine hoont	a dog	**eine Maus** ine a mouse	a mouse
eine Frau ine a fraow	a woman		

Klaus has aready guessed what three people are. *Du bist* [doo bist] means "you are".

Can you say in German what he will say to all the others when he guesses what they are pretending to be?

Ich bin ...

Ich bin ...

Ich bin ...

Ich bin ...

Was sollte man
vass zollta mun
mit einer riesigen
mit ine a reezign
Maus nie tun?
mouse nee toon

Sich streiten.
zikh shtryten

Du bist eine Katze!

Ja, ich bin eine Katze.

Du bist dran

What are you?

You could play a Guess who? game in German with friends.

How to play:

Choose someone to be the first guesser. All the other players act out what they would like to be.

The guesser shouts out in German when he guesses someone, using *du bist* [doo bist] then what he thinks you are.

Say *ja* [yah] and then what you are in German if he is right. (Remember, *ich bin* means "I am"). You are then the next guesser.

Say *nein* [nine] if he is wrong and continue until someone is guessed correctly.

Once you have been a guesser, you must think of something else to be (or everyone will know at once what you are).

47

Joke: What must you never do with an enormous mouse? Argue.

Weather

Nobody in the Strudel family can agree about where to go on a rainy day. So Uli has stayed at the chalet with Karin and the twins while the others have all set off on different daytrips.

Which of the Strudels are joking when they phone Karin to tell her what the weather is like where they are? Use the word list to find out.

Can you say out loud in German what those who are joking should be saying to Karin?

Word list

wie ist das Wetter? vee ist dass vetter	what's the weather like?
es ist schön ess ist shern	it's fine
es regnet ess raygnet	it's raining
es ist kalt ess ist kullt	it's cold
es ist sehr warm ess ist zair vahrm	it's hot
es ist windig ess ist vindikh	it's windy
es schneit ess shnite	it's snowing
hier here	here

48

Names

Karin
kahrin

Helga
hellga

Du bist dran

Wie ist das Wetter? [vee ist dass vetter]. What's the weather like where you are at the moment? Can you say it in German?

You could write a postcard in German telling someone what the weather is like. Use the word lists, the pictures and the postcard Silvia has written to her friend, Helga, to see how to say all the words you need.

If you are writing to a boy or man you write *lieber.*

This means "How are you?"

> Liebe Helga,
> Wie geht's?
> Es ist sehr warm hier.
> Viele Grüße,
> Silvia.

This means "love from". German people often write this at the end of a card or letter.

Word list

lieber/liebe leeber,leeba	dear..
wie geht's? vee gates	how are you?
sehr zair	very
viele Grüße feela grewssa	love from

49

Silvia's body game

When everyone returns to the house, the rain is still pouring down. Silvia has made up a game for everyone to play.

Why don't you make Silvia's body game and play it too?

You will need: a dice, paper, pencils or felt tip pens.

Du bist dran.

der Körper

This is the shape you start with.

Word list

du bist dran — your turn
doo bist dran
ich habe gewonnen — I've won
ikh hahba gavonnen

⚀	ein Fuß
⚁	eine Hand
⚂	ein Arm
⚃	ein Bein
⚄	der Kopf
⚅	der Körper

The idea of the game is to be the first to complete a drawing of a person. Take turns throwing the dice. You must throw a 6 and shout out *der Körper* [dair kerper] to start. You can then draw the body.

Use the key above to see which numbers you must throw to add the other parts.

Say the name of each body part in German as you draw it. If you already have the part for any number you throw, pass the dice to the next player. (Remember that you need 2 arms, legs, feet and hands.)

You cannot add hands and feet before the arms and legs.

The first player to complete their person shouts out *der Mensch* [dair mensh], and is the winner. *Ich habe gewonnen* [ikh hahba gavonnen] means "I've won".

Picture list

der Mensch
dair mensh
person

der Kopf
dair kopf
head

die Hand
dee hunt
hand

der Arm
dair arm
arm

der Körper
dair kerper
body

das Bein
dass bine
leg

der Fuß
dair fooss
foot

Der Mensch! Ich habe gewonnen.

50

Making faces

You can play the same game with faces. Cut out lots of eyes, eyebrows, noses, ears and mouths from old magazines. Stick these on paper plates to make up your faces.

You will need:
paper plates, old magazines, scissors, glue and felt tip pens.

Play in the same way as the body game. You must throw a 6 and shout out *die Haare* [dee hahra] to start. Draw on the hair with felt tips.

Check the number on the dice against the key below to see which parts you can then stick on. Remember to say the name of each part in German as you stick it on.

die Haare

· der Mund
·· die Nase
··· eine Augenbraue
···· ein Ohr
····· ein Auge
······ die Haare

The first one to complete their head with hair, 2 eyes, 2 eyebrows, 2 ears, a nose and a mouth shouts *der Kopf* [dair kopf], which means "the head", and is the winner.

Der Kopf! Ich habe gewonnen.

Song

Here is a song about faces and bodies to sing in German. Point to each part of the body as you sing about it. You can find the tune on page 64.

Kopf und Schultern, Knie und Zehe, Knie und Zehe,
kopf oont shooltern k neeya oont tsaya k neeya oont tsaya
Kopf und Schultern, Knie und Zehe, Knie und Zehe,
kopf oont shooltern k neeya oont tsaya k neeya oont tsaya
Augen, Nase, Ohren und Mund,
owgn nahza aw ren oont moont
Kopf und Schultern, Knie und Zehe, Knie und Zehe.
kopf oont shooltern k neeya oont tsaya k neeya oont tsaya

Head and shoulders, knees and toes, knees and toes,
Head and shoulders, knees and toes, knees and toes,
Eyes, nose, ears and mouth,
Head and shoulders, knees and toes, knees and toes.

Car game

The next day dawns bright and sunny and the Strudels pile into the car to go to the fair along the coast. It is a long drive so they play a guessing game to pass the time.

The game is to give clues to somewhere and everyone has to guess where this place is.

Es gibt [ess gipt] means "there is" or "there are".

Frau Strudel starts. She says that at the place she is thinking of *Es gibt das Meer, Sand, Steine* [ess gipt das mair zunt shtyna]. This means "there is the sea, sand, rocks...". Markus guesses *Es ist der Strand* [ess ist dair shtrunt] which means "it's the beach". He is right so now it is his turn.

Use the word list to help you see what the others are thinking of. Say the clues out loud, then shout out the right answer from the answer list.

Names

Frau Strudel   Mrs. Strudel
fraow shtroodel

Du bist dran
You can play this game too. Just say *es gibt* [ess gipt] and a few of the words on the word list to describe the place you are thinking about and wait until someone guesses correctly - in German of course.

Word list

es gibt	there is, there are	die Blumen	flowers
ess gipt		dee bloomn	
es ist	it is	die Pralinen	chocolates
ess ist		dee prah leenen	
das Meer	sea	die Matrosen	sailors
dass mair		dee matrawzen	
das Geld	money	die Schaukeln	swings
dass gelt		dee shaowkeln	
der Sand	sand	die Vögel	birds
dair zunt		dee fergl	
die Theke	(shop, store) counter	die Steine	rocks
dee tayka		dee shtyna	
die Bänke	benches	die Straßen	streets
dee benka		dee shtrahssen	
die Boote	boats	die Autos	car
dee bawta		dee owtaws	
die Gebäude	buildings	die Bäume	trees
dee geboyda		dee boyma	

Remember that in German, naming words (nouns) usually change when they mean more than one of something (plural). Most words on this list are plurals. You can see how to say the words for one of each thing (singular) on pages 62 and 63.

Answer list

das Geschäft	shop, store
dass gesheft	
der Wald	forest
dair valt	
der Strand	beach
dair shtrunt	
die Stadt	town
dee shtut	
der Park	park
dair park	
der Hafen	port
dair hahfen	

53

Joke: What's big, grey and goes "ooooo"? An ele-phantom.

Funny shapes

When they reach the fair, the Strudels go into the Hall of Mirrors. The mirrors make people look very different from their normal shape and size.

Silvia's reflection is too big. Markus says, *Sie ist zu groß* [zee ist tsoo grawss], which means "she is too big".

Can you say what is wrong with each person's reflection? Use the word list to find out the words for tall, small, fat and thin.

If it is a boy or a man, say *er ist* [air ist]. If it is a girl or a woman, say *sie ist* [zee ist].

Picture list

Describing words (adjectives) in German usually change their spelling when they come before a naming word (noun). On this page they don't.

klein	small, short	dick	fat
klyne		dick	
groß	big, tall	dünn	thin
grawss		doon	

Word list

ich bin	I am	sie ist	she is
ikh bin		zee ist	
zu	too	er ist	he is
tsoo		air ist	

Du bist dran

Are you tall or small? To answer, say *ich bin* [ikh bin] which means "I am" and then the right word from the word list.

Describe your family too, using *er ist* [air ist] for males and *sie ist* [zee ist] for females.

55

Joke: What's black and white and very noisy? A penguin playing the trumpet.
(In German, you don't say the "and" in "black and white". It's just *schwarzweiß*.)

Hot work

On the way home from the fair, the Strudels' car breaks down. Setting off on foot, they all realize how hungry or thirsty they are.

Can you see which roads Karin and the twins, Josefina, Oma and Herr Strudel should take to get what they want?

Ich habe Hunger [ikh hahba hoonger] means "I'm hungry". *Ich habe Durst* [ikh hahba doorst] means "I'm thirsty".

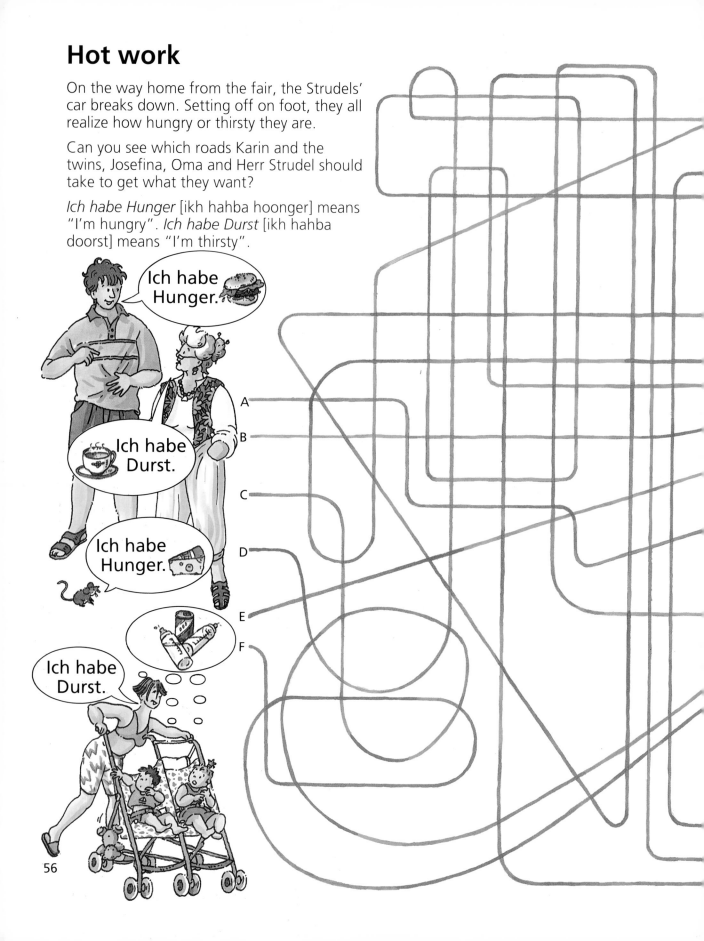

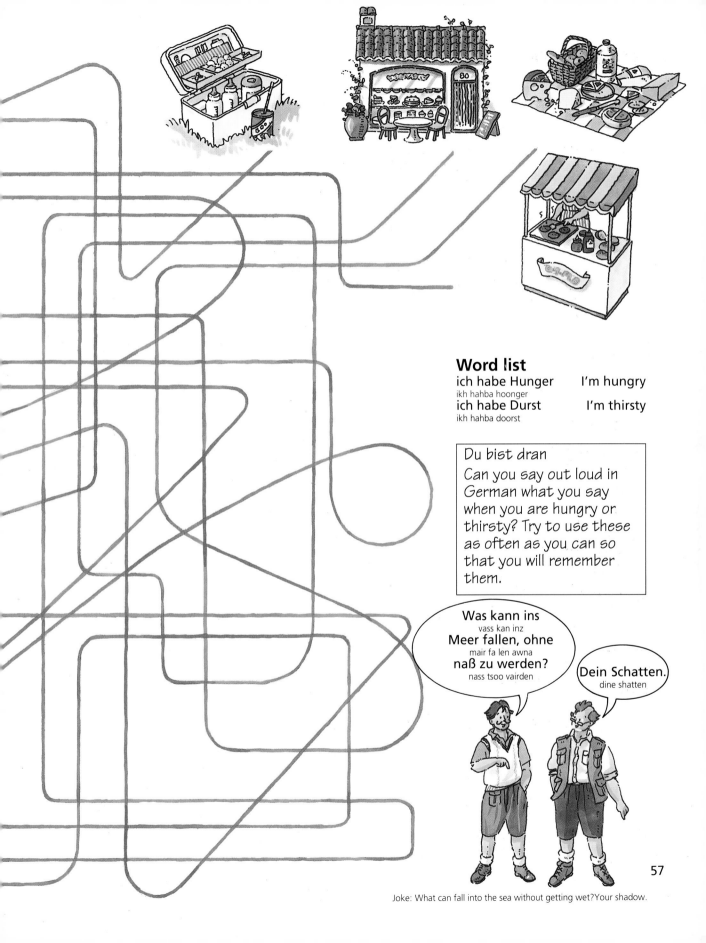

Word list

ich habe Hunger   I'm hungry
ikh hahba hoonger

ich habe Durst   I'm thirsty
ikh hahba doorst

Du bist dran
Can you say out loud in German what you say when you are hungry or thirsty? Try to use these as often as you can so that you will remember them.

Was kann ins
vass kan inz
Meer fallen, ohne
mair fa len awna
naß zu werden?
nass tsoo vairden

Dein Schatten.
dine shatten

57

Joke: What can fall into the sea without getting wet? Your shadow.

Snapshots

The twins have got hold of some of Markus's photographs and have torn them into pieces. Oma Strudel has offered to stick the mixed-up pieces back together. Markus has written a note to help her. Read it to see what Silvia, Onkel Helmut and Tante Ilse are wearing in the photographs. *Trägt* [traykt] after someone's name means "is wearing" in German. Can you help Oma see which six pieces belong to each photograph?

Markus's note

Onkel Helmut trägt einen Mantel, ein Hemd, eine Hose und Schuhe.

Silvia trägt einen Badeanzug, einen Hut und Stiefel.

Tante Ilse trägt eine Sonnenbrille, einen Rock, einen Pullover und Socken.

Use the word list to read out loud in German what each person is wearing.

Word list

schade! *shahda*	what a pity!
..trägt.. *traykt*	..is wearing..
ich trage *ikh trahga*	I am wearing
ein Rock* *ine rock*	a skirt
ein Pullover* *ine pull awver*	a pullover
ein Badeanzug* *ine bahda an tsoog*	a swimsuit
eine Sonnenbrille *zonnen brilla*	sunglasses
eine Hose *ine a hawza*	trousers
ein Mantel* *ine muntle*	a coat
ein Hemd* *ine hemt*	a shirt
ein Hut* *ine hoot*	a hat

Socken *zokken*	socks
Schuhe *shooa*	shoes
Stiefel *shteefle*	boots
und *oont*	and
was trägst du? *vass traykst doo*	what are you wearing?

*Did you notice the word *einen* before some of the words in Markus's note? The word for "a" changes from *ein* to *einen* with *der* (masculine) words. These are marked * on the word list.

Names

Onkel Helmut *onkel helmoot* — Uncle Helmut

Du bist dran

Was trägst du? [*vass traykst doo*]. What are you wearing? Say *ich trage* [*ikh trahga*] and then your clothes. Can you describe what your family or friends are wearing? Here are some more clothes words that you may need.

ein Kleid *ine klyte*	a dress
ein T-Shirt *ine tee shirt*	a T-shirt
Shorts *shorts*	shorts

59

Joke: What's green and goes tic-toc? A clockwork cucumber.

Going home

It's time for the Strudels to say goodbye to all the people they have met at the beach.

On the way home, they stop to buy little presents and souvenirs. Uli already knows what he wants to buy - the green flippers.

Can you see what everyone else would like? Use the word list to help you say in German how each person will ask for what he or she wants. Look at the guide opposite to see how to say the describing words on their own.

Word list

ich möchte... ikh merkhta	I would like...
die grünen Flossen dee grewnen flossen	the green flippers
die grüne Marionette dee grewna marionetta	the green puppet
die braune Marionette dee browna marionetta	the brown puppet
das lila Portemonnaie dass leelah port monnay	the purple(money)purse
die weißen Stiefel dee vyssen shteefle	the white boots
die gelben Blumen dee gelben bloomn	the yellow flowers
die roten Blumen dee rawtn bloomn	the red flowers
die blaue Tasche dee blaowa tasha	the blue bag
die schwarze Trommel dee shvahrtsa trommel	the black drum
bitte bitta	please
Auf Wiedersehen owf veederzane	goodbye

60

Song

Here is a song about a rainbow to sing in German.
You can see what all the words mean on page 64.

Rot und ro - sa und gelb und grün, vi - o - lett, li - la und blau,
rawt oont raw za oont gelp oont grewn vee aw let lee lah oont blaow

bun - ter Re - gen - bo - gen, schö - ner Bo - gen, mei - ne Welt'st nicht grau. Im
boon ter ray gn baw gn sher ner baw gn my na velts nikht graow im

Som - mer ist es grün, die Fel - der voll - er gelb, und die Wol - ken am Him - mel weiß,
zom mer ist ess grewn dee fell der foll er gelp oont dee vol ken am him mel vice

ro - te Ro - sen blü - hen, Far - ben glü - hen, und es wächst viel Mais.
raw ta raw zen blew en far ben glew en oont ess vext feel mice

Du bist dran
Which object would you most like to have? Can you ask for it in German?

Guide

rot
rawt
blau
blaow
gelb
gelp
rosa
rawza
grün
grewn
braun
brown
lila
leelah
schwarz
shvahrts
weiß
vice

Did you notice that the describing words on the word list are different from the ones above? In German, describing words (adjectives) usually change their spelling when they come before naming words (nouns).

Word list (part 2)

Here is a list of all the German words and phrases** used in this part of the book in alphabetical order. Use the list either to check quickly what a word means, or to test yourself. Cover up any German or English word or phrase and see if you can say its translation. Remember that most words change slightly when you are talking about more than one thing (plural).

German	Pronunciation	English
acht	akht	eight
Angelrute (die)	ang el roota	fishing rod
Arm (der)	arm	arm
auf	owf	on (top of)
Auf Wiedersehen	owf veederzane	goodbye
Auge (das)	owga	eye
Augenbraue (die)	owgn braowa	eyebrow
Auto (das),	owtaw,	car,
Autos (die)	owtaws	cars
Badeanzug (der)	bahda an tsoog	swimsuit
Bahnhof (der)	bahn hawf	station
Ball (der)	bal	ball
Bank (die)	bank	bench
Bänke (die)	benka	benches
Bauernhof (der)	baowan hawf	farm
Baum (der)	baowm	tree
Bäume (die)	boyma	trees
bei den Strudels	by dane shtroodels	(at) the Strudels' home
Bein (das)	bine	leg
Bett (das)	bet	bed
bitte	bitta	please
blau	blaow	blue
Blume, Blumen (die)	blooma, bloomn	flower (s)
Boot (das),	bawt,	boat,
Boote (die)	bawta	boats
braun	brown	brown
Burg (die)	boorg	castle
Café (das)	ka fay	café
Campingplatz (der)	kemping pluts	campsite
da ist er, sie, es	dah ist air,zee,ess	there it is
der, die, das	dair, dee, dass	the
dick	dick	fat
drei	dry	three
du bist	doo bist	you are
du bist dran	doo bist dran	your turn
dünn	doon*	thin
Eimer (der)	eyemer	bucket
ein, eine, einen	ine, ine a, ine n	a/an/one
eins	ine ts	one
62 **einverstanden**	ine fer shtanden	OK, agreed

German	Pronunciation	English
er heißt	air hyste	he is called
er ist	air ist	he is
es gibt	ess gipt	there is/there are
es ist	ess ist	it is
es ist kalt	ess ist kullt	it's cold
es ist schön	ess ist shern	it's fine
es ist sehr warm	ess ist zair vahrm	it's hot
es ist windig	ess ist vindikh	it's windy
es regnet	ess raygnet	it's raining
es schneit	ess shnite	it's snowing
Feld (das)	felt	field
Fernseher (der)	fairn zayer	television
Flossen (die)	flossen	flippers
Frau (die)	fraow	Mrs., woman
Fuchs (der)	fooks*	fox
Füchse (die)	fooksa*	foxes
fünf	foonf*	five
Fuß (der)	fooss	foot
Gebäude (das),(die)	geboyda	building, building
gelb	gelp	yellow
Geld (das)	gelt	money
Geschäft (das)	gesheft	shop, store
groß	grawss	big, tall
grün	grewn	green
Guten Abend	gootn ah bnd	good evening
Guten Tag	gootn tahg	hello
Haare (die)	hahra	hair
Hafen (der)	hahfen	port
Hallo	hullaw	hi
Hand (die)	hunt	hand
Handtuch (das)	hunt tookh	towel
Haus (das)	howss	house
Häuschen (das)	hoyss khen	cottage
Hemd (das)	hemt	shirt
Herr	hair	Mr.
hier	here	here
hinter	hinter	behind
Hirsch (der)	heersh	stag
Hirsche (die)	heersha	stags
Hose (die)	hawza	trousers
Hund (der)	hoont*	dog
Hut (der)	hoot	hat
ich bin	ikh bin	I am
ich habe Durst	ikh hahba doorst	I'm thirsty
ich habe gewonnen	ikh hahba gavonnen	I've won
ich habe Hunger	ikh hahba hoonger*	I'm hungry
ich heiße	ikh hyssa	I am called
ich möchte	ikh merkhta	I would like
ich spreche Deutsch	ikh shprekha doytsh	I speak German
ich trage	ikh trahga	I am wearing
in	in	in
ja	yah	yes

* The 'u' sound in these words is like the 'u' in 'put'.
** Except those in the jokes and songs, which are translated on the pages or on the answer page.

German	Pronunciation	English
Jahre alt	yahra ult	*years old*
Junge (der)	yoonga*	*boy*
Kaninchen (das),(die)	ka neen khn	*rabbit, rabbits*
Katze, Katzen (die)	katsa, katsn	*cat, cats*
Kirche (die)	keerkha	*church*
Kleid (das)	klyte	*dress*
klein	klyne	*small, short*
König (der)	kernikh	*king*
Königin (die)	kernig in	*queen*
Kopf (der)	kopf	*head*
Korb (der)	korp	*basket*
Körper (der)	kerper	*body*
lieber, liebe	leeber, leeba	*dear*
lila	leelah	*purple*
Mädchen (das)	mate khen	*girl*
Mann (der)	mun	*man*
Mantel (der)	muntle	*coat*
Marionette (die)	marionetta	*puppet*
Markt (der)	markt	*market*
Matrose (der)	matrawza	*sailor*
Matrosen (die)	matrawzen	*sailors*
Mauer (die)	maower	*wall*
Maus, Mäuse (die)	mouse, moyza	*mouse, mice*
Meer (das)	mair	*sea*
Mensch (der)	mensh	*person*
Mund (der)	moont*	*mouth*
Nase (die)	nahza	*nose*
neben	naybn	*beside*
nein	nine	*no*
Nest (das)	nest	*nest*
Nester (die)	nester	*nests*
neun	noyn	*nine*
Ohr (das)	or	*ear*
Ohren (die)	aw ren	*ears*
Oma (die)	awma	*grandma*
Papierkorb (der)	pupeerkorp	*wastepaper basket*
Park (der)	park	*park*
Pferd (das)	pfairt	*horse*
Pflanze (die)	pfluntsa	*plant*
Pralinen (die)	prah leenan	*chocolates*
Portemonnaie (das)	port monnay	*(money)purse*
Pullover (der)	pull awver	*pullover*
Radio (das)	rah dee aw	*radio*
Regenschirm (der)	ray gun sheerm	*umbrella*
Rock (der)	rock	*skirt*
rosa	rawza	*pink*
rot	rawt	*red*
Sand (der)	zunt	*sand*
schade!	shahda	*what a pity!*
Schaukel (die)	shaowkel	*swing*
Schaukeln (die)	shaowkeln	*swings*
Schlange(die)	shlunga	*snake,*
Schlangen (die)	shlungn	*snakes*
Schrank (der)	shrunk	*cupboard*
Schmetterling (der)	shmetterling	*butterfly*
Schmetterlinge (die)	shmetterlinga	*butterflies*
Schuh (der)	shoo	*shoe*
Schule (die)	shoola	*school*
schwarz	shvahrts	*black*
sechs	zex	*six*
See (der)	zay	*lake*
sehr	zair	*very*
Shorts (die)	shorts	*shorts*
sieben	zeebn	*seven*
sie ist	zee ist	*she is*
Socke (die)	zokka	*sock*
Sofa (das)	zawfah	*sofa*
Sonnenbrille (die)	zonnen brilla	*(a pair of) sunglasses*
Spiegel (der)	shpeegl	*mirror*
Spiel (das), Spiele(die)	shpeel, shpeela	*game, games*
Stadt (die)	shtut	*town*
Stein (der), Steine(die)	shtyne, shtyna	*rock, rocks*
Stiefel (der)	shteefle	*boot*
Strand (der)	shtrunt	*beach*
Straße (die)	shtrahssa	*street*
Straßen (die)	shtrahssan	*streets*
Tasche (die)	tasha	*bag*
Theke (die)	tayka	*(shop)counter*
Tisch (der)	tish	*table*
Tor (das)	tawr	*gate*
..trägt	traykt	*.. is wearing*
Trommel (die)	trommel	*drum*
T-Shirt (das)	tee shirt	*T-shirt*
und	oont*	*and*
unter	oonter*	*under*
viele Grüße	feela grewssa	*love from*
vier	feer	*four*
Vogel (der), Vögel(die)	fawgl, fergl	*bird, birds*
vor	fore	*in front of*
Vorhang (der)	fore hung	*curtain*
Wald (der)	valt	*forest*
Wäschekorb (der)	veshakorp	*laundry basket*
was ist	vass ist	*what is*
was trägst du?	vass traykst doo	*what are you wearing?*
weiß	vice	*white*
wie alt bist du?	vee ult bist doo	*how old are you?*
wie geht's?	vee gates	*how are you?*
wie heißt du?	vee hyste doo	*what are you called?*
wie ist das Wetter?	vee ist dass vetter	*what's the weather like?*
wieviele?	vee feela	*how many?*
Windmühle (die)	vintmoola	*windmill*
wo ist	vaw ist	*where is*
zehn	tsayn	*ten*
Zeitung (die)	tsy toong*	*newspaper*
Zelt (das)	tsellt	*tent*
zu	tsoo	*too*
zwei	tsvy	*two*

Answers (part 2)

PAGE 35

Here is how each word changes:
Add ¨ to *Vogel* to make *Vögel*.
Add ¨ and an "e" to *Ball* to make *Bälle*.
Add "n" to *Katze* to make *Katzen*.
Add "er" to *Nest* to make *Nester*.
Add ¨ and "er" to *Handtuch* to make *Handtücher*.
Add "s" to *Auto* to make *Autos*.
Mädchen stays the same.
Add "en" to *Ohr* to make *Ohren*.
Add "e" to *Bein* to make *Beine*.
Der, die and *das* all become *die*.

PAGE 38-39

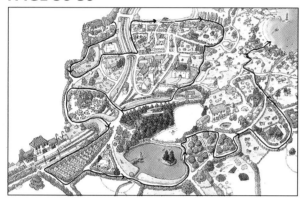

PAGE 40-41

Uli has counted correctly.
Es gibt sieben Bäume.
Es gibt ein Nest.
Es gibt zehn Blumen.

PAGE 42-43

Markus is saying *Ich bin acht Jahre alt.*
Uli is saying *Wie alt bist du?*
Silvia is saying *Ich bin sieben Jahre alt.*
Either of the twins would say *Ich bin ein Jahr alt.*

PAGE 44-45

The box that Uli finds is in the right place.

PAGE 46-47

Klaus will say: *Du bist ein Hund; Du bist eine Katze; Du bist ein Junge; Du bist eine Frau; Du bist eine Königin; Du bist ein Pferd; Du bist ein Vogel; Du bist ein Mann.*

PAGE 48-49

Oma is joking. She should say *Es ist windig.*

Herr Strudel is joking. He should say *Es regnet.*

Onkel Helmut is joking. He should say *Es ist sehr warm.*

PAGE 50-51

PAGE 52-53

A. *Es ist der Strand.*
B. *Es ist der Hafen.*
C. *Es ist das Geschäft.*
D. *Es ist die Stadt.*
E. *Es ist der Park.*
F. *Es ist der Wald.*

PAGE 56-57

Karin and the twins take road F,
Josefina takes road C,
Oma takes road E,
Herr Strudel takes road B.

PAGE 58-59

Silvia:	Tante Ilse:	Onkel Helmut:
F G I M O R	B D E J L Q	A C H K N P

PAGE 60-61

Katja: *Ich möchte das lila Portemonnaie.*
Tante Ilse: *Ich möchte die blaue Tasche.*
Herr Strudel: *Ich möchte die roten Blumen.*
Frau Strudel: *Ich möchte die gelben Blumen.*
Onkel Helmut: *Ich möchte die schwarze Trommel.*
Markus: *Ich möchte die braune Marionette.*
Silvia: *Ich möchte die grüne Marionette.*
Oma Strudel: *Ich möchte die weißen Stiefel.*

Here are the words of the song in English:

Red and pink and yellow and green,
Violet, purple and blue,
Colourful rainbow, beautiful arc,
My world's not grey.
In summer it is green
The fields full of yellow
And the clouds in the sky are white.
Red roses are blooming
Colours are glowing
And there's lots of corn growing.

First German

PART 3: AT SCHOOL

Kathy Gemmell and Jenny Tyler
Illustrated by Sue Stitt
Designed by Diane Thistlethwaite

Consultant: Sandy Walker

CONTENTS
(part 3)

In this part of the book, the Strudel children are back at school. They are going to help you learn even more German.

Word lists

Don't forget to use the word lists to tell you what the German words mean.

Hallo
hullaw

Make sure you read the little letters carefully to see how to say each word.

Guten Tag
gootn tahg

Word list

Guten Tag gootn tahg	hello
Hallo hullaw	hi
Entschuldigung entshooldigoong	sorry
du bist dran doo bist dran	your turn
wie geht's? vee gates	how are you?
wo ist die Katze? vaw ist dee katsa	where is the cat?
sehr gut, danke zair goot dunka	very well, thank you

Remember to try and listen to German people speaking and copy what they say. Here are more clues to help you say some of the sounds which are different from English.

The "ei" in German sounds like "eye". Say *ich heiße* [ikh hyssa], which means "I am called".

Say the German "w" like the English "v". Try saying *wo ist* [vaw ist] which means "where is".

The "ng" in German sounds like the "ng" in "singer". Remember that "sch" sounds like the English "sh". See if you can say *Entschuldigung* [entshooldigoong] which is the word for "sorry" in German.

Try to say out loud what each person on this page is saying.

Can you find Josefina the mouse on every double page in this part of the book?

Wie geht's?
vee gates

Sehr
zair
gut, danke.
goot dunka

Wo ist
vaw ist
die Katze?
dee katsa

Entschuldigung
entshooldigoong

Games

Here is a game you can play with *der*, *die* and *das* words. Count up the number of *der* words (masculine), *die* words (feminine) and *das* words (neuter) on each page.

Say all the *der* words out loud, then shut the book and see how many you can remember. Do the same with the *die* and *das* words.

You could play this with a friend. Do it one page at a time. Take turns saying *der* words until one of you can't remember any more. Score a point for each word you can remember after your friend has given up.

Do the same with *die* and *das* words. The winner is the one to score the most points.

Du bist dran
There are *du bist dran* boxes in this part of the book as well. Look out for them for extra things to do in German.

Don't forget to look for joke bubbles on some of the pages.

In the classroom

Silvia and Markus Strudel are back at school today. There is a new boy in their class. He introduces himself by saying *Ich heiße Jörg* [ikh hyssa yerg]. *Ich heiße* is how you say "I am called" or "my name is" in German.

Can you help the children introduce themselves to Jörg, by saying what's in each speech bubble? Use the word list to help you.

Can you work out which way Jörg should go so that he only passes each of them once and ends up at the teacher's desk?

Names

Strudel	**Uli**
shtroodel	oolee
Ziffer	**Jörg**
tsiffer	yerg
Rainer	**Anke**
ryner	unka
Silvia	**Petra**
zilveeya	paytra
Markus	**Klaus**
mahrkoos	klaowss
Katja	**Rudi**
katya	roody

Word list

wie heißt du?	what's your name?
vee hyste doo	
ich heiße	I am called/my name is
ikh hyssa	
er heißt	he is called
air hyste	
sie heißt	she is called
zee hyste	
meine Mutter	my mother
myna rnootter	
mein Vater	my father
myne fahter	
mein Bruder	my brother
mine brooder	
meine Schwester	my sister
myna shvester	
Herr	Mr.
hair	
Frau	Mrs.
fraow	
Oma	Granny
awma	

68

Happy families

Can you match up the people in the column on the right with the person who is talking about them? Use the word list see what all the words mean.

What is Markus's sister called?
What is Silvia's father called?
Can you answer in German? *Er heißt* [air hyste] means "he is called" and *sie heißt* [zee hyste] means "she is called".

Du bist dran
Wie heißt du? [vee hyste doo].
What's your name? Try and introduce yourself and your family in German, using the words on this page to help you.

69

How are you?

Look at the picture to see how everyone is this morning.

To ask how someone is in German you say *Wie geht's?* [vee gates] which means, "How are you?"

Frau Ziffer is talking to someone who is saying "I'm very well, thank you," in German. Use the word list to see how to say this out loud.

Where are they?

Can you spot the following people in the picture?

Someone who has toothache?

Someone with a headache?

Someone who is saying "My leg hurts"?

Someone with a tummy-ache?

Someone who feels all right?

Use the word list to help you say out loud in German what each person is saying.

Can you spot the words for arm, leg, hand and foot on this page?

der Arm
dair arm

der Fuß
dair fooss

das Bein
dass bine

At home

Here are some of the Strudel family at home. They should be saying how they feel but the speech bubbles have all been mixed up. Can you say what each person should be saying?

Frau Strudel

Oma Strudel

Word list

German	Pronunciation	English
Guten Tag	gootn tahg	good morning, hello
danke	dunka	thank you
wie geht's?	vee gates	how are you?
(es geht mir) sehr gut	ess gate meer zair goot	I'm very well
ich habe Zahnweh	ikh hahba tsahnvay	I have toothache
ich habe Kopfweh	ikh hahba kopfvay	I have a headache
ich habe Bauchweh	ikh hahba baowkhvay	I have a tummy-ache
mein Bein tut mir weh	mine bine toot meer vay	my leg hurts
Oma	awma	Granny
Frau	fraow	Mrs.
Herr	hair	Mr.

Der, die and das

Did you notice that some of the words have *der*, *die* or *das* before them? Remember that these all mean "the" in German.

All naming words (nouns) are masculine, feminine or neuter in German. You use *der* for masculine words, *die* for feminine words and *das* for neuter words. Make sure you learn words with their *der, die* or *das,* as you cannot guess which is which.

Dont forget that in German, all nouns begin with a capital letter.

Du bist dran
Wie geht's? [vee gates].

How do you feel at the moment? Look at what everyone in the cloakroom is saying to help you say how you feel today. Ask your family and friends how they are in German. You could draw pictures of them and give them German speech bubbles.

Counting

Can you help Silvia with her counting? Look at the first picture to see her counting the books. Count the things in the other pictures in the same way, starting with *eins* [ine ts], *zwei* [tsvy].

How many things are in each picture? Answer by saying *es gibt* [ess gipt] and then the number of things you have counted. Use the word list to see how to say all the words.

> Eins, zwei, drei, vier, fünf, sechs, sieben, acht, neun, zehn.

> Es gibt zehn Bücher.

Bücher

Pflanzen

Regenschirme

Number list

eins	one	fünf	five	acht	eight
ine ts		foonf		akht	
zwei	two	sechs	six	neun	nine
tsvy		zex		noyn	
drei	three	sieben	seven	zehn	ten
dry		zeebn		tsain	
vier	four				
feer					

Word list

es gibt	there is, there are	die Bücher	books
ess gipt		dee boosher	
die Geschenke	presents	die Hüte	hats
dee geshenka		dee hoota	
die Bleistifte	pencils	die Pflanzen	plants
dee bly shtifta		dee pfluntsn	
die Regenschirme umbrellas			
dee raygn sheerma			

Die means "the" when you are talking about more than one object (plural). You don't say *die* after a number.

Du bist dran

Look for things around your house to count. Count them in German. If you want to continue past ten, here are the numbers up to twenty:

elf	eleven	sechzehn	sixteen
elf		zekh tsain	
zwölf	twelve	siebzehn	seventeen
tsverlf		zeep tsain	
dreizehn	thirteen	achtzehn	eighteen
dry tsain		akht tsain	
vierzehn	fourteen	neunzehn	nineteen
feer tsain		noyn tsain	
fünfzehn	fifteen	zwanzig	twenty
foonf tsain		tsvan tsikh	

Geschenke

Bleistifte

Song

Here are the first three verses of a German song. Can you sing it right up to *Zehn Hund' wollten spiel'n...* using all the numbers up to ten in German? Sing it to the tune of "One man went to mow". You can see the tune on page 96 if you don't know it.

Ein Hund wollte spiel'n, wollte Fußball spielen,
ine hoont vollta shpeeln vollta foossbal shpeelen
Ein Hund und sein Herr wollten Fußball spielen.
ine hoont oont zine hair vollten foossbal shpeelen

Zwei Hund' wollten spiel'n, wollten
tsvy hoont vollten shpeeln vollten
 Fußball spielen,
 foossbal shpeelen
Zwei Hund', ein Hund und sein Herr wollten
tsvy hoont ine hoont oont zine hair vollten
 Fußball spielen.
 foossbal shpeelen

Drei Hund' wollten spiel'n, wollten
dry hoont vollten shpeeln vollten
 Fußball spielen,
 foossbal shpeelen
Drei Hund', zwei Hund', ein Hund und sein Herr
dry hoont tsvy hoont ine hoont oont zine hair
 wollten Fußball spielen.
 vollten foossbal shpeelen

Here is what the song means in English:

One dog wanted to play, wanted to play football,
One dog and his master wanted to play football.
Two dogs wanted to play ... etc.

Was ergibt sich, wenn
vass airgipt zikh ven
man einen Elefanten mit
mun ine n ellay funten mit
einem Känguruh kreuzt?
ine m kengooroo kroytst

Ganz große
gants grawssa
Löcher überall in
lersher ooberull in
Australien.
owsstrahlian

Hüte

Joke: What do you get if you cross an elephant with a kangaroo?
Great big holes all over Australia.

Days of the week

Silvia and Markus both have timetables to tell them which subject their group will be doing each day.

Using Silvia and Markus's timetables, can you see which day it is in each of the pictures? Say *es ist* [ess ist] which means "it is" and then the day of the week. Look at the word list to see how to say each of the days.

Silvia	
Montag	Zeichnen
Dienstag	Deutsch
Mittwoch	Sport
Donnerstag	Englisch
Freitag	Musik
Samstag	das
Sonntag	Wochenende

Markus	
Montag	Sport
Dienstag	Zeichnen
Mittwoch	Englisch
Donnerstag	Deutsch
Freitag	Musik
Samstag	das
Sonntag	Wochenende

Word list

es ist ess ist	it is
Montag mawntahg	Monday
Dienstag deenstahg	Tuesday
Mittwoch mitvokh	Wednesday
Donnerstag donnerstahg	Thursday
Freitag frytahg	Friday
Samstag zamstahg	Saturday
Sonntag zonntag	Sunday
das Wochenende dass vokhen enda	weekend
Deutsch doytch	German
Englisch eng glish	English
Sport shport	sport
Zeichnen tsykhnen	drawing, art
Musik moozeek	music
heute hoyta	today

How many times can you spot the word *das* on these two pages? Remember, *das* is how you say "the" when you are talking about neuter words. For masculine words, "the" is *der* and for feminine words "the" is *die*.

74

Indoor hopscotch

Hopscotch in German is called *Himmel-und-Hölle* [himmel oont herla]. Here is a type of hopscotch you can play indoors.

Using the word list to help you, write out the days of the week in German on seven squares of paper (each one large enough to put your foot on).

Herr Ober, in
hair awber in
meiner Suppe ist
myner zooppa ist
eine Spinne!
ine a shpinna

Es tut mir sehr
ess toot meer zair
leid, die Fliege hat
lyte dee fleega hat
heute frei.
hoyta fry

The aim of the game is to collect as many of the paper squares as possible.

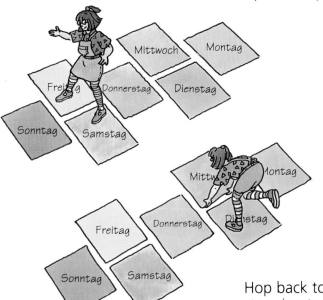

Arrange the seven squares on the floor like this with *Montag* (Monday) nearest you:

Stand about 1m (3ft) away from the first square. Throw a coin onto any one of the squares. Say that day out loud in German, using *es ist* and then the day. (If the stone lands between or outside the squares, throw again.)

Then hop up the squares, putting one foot on each of the squares that are side by side, without stepping on the square with the stone on it. You can only hop once on the top square (*Sonntag*).

Hop back to the beginning, stopping to pick up the coin and its paper square on the way.

Continue until you have thrown the coin onto all the squares. Remember to say each of the days out loud in German. You will have to hop over wider and wider gaps as you pick up more and more squares.

You can play this game by yourself, or with a friend. If you are playing with a friend, take turns to throw. The winner is the one with the most paper squares at the end.

Joke: Waiter, there's a spider in my soup!
I'm sorry, sir, it's the fly's day off.

Du bist dran
Can you say in German what day it is today? "Today" in German is *heute* [hoyta]. Say *es ist heute* [ess ist hoyta] then the day. Try saying what day it is in German every morning for a week.

Putting on a play

Everyone is getting ready for the school play. Most of the children seem to have lost something in the piles of clothes lying around the stage.

To say, "I have lost," in German, you say *ich habe* [ikh hahba], then what you have lost and then you say *verloren* [fair lawren].

So to say, "I have lost my watch," you would say *Ich habe meine Armbanduhr verloren* [ikh hahba myna armbandoor fair lawren].

Using the word list to help you, can you say in German what each child is saying?

Can you find all of the lost objects somewhere in the picture?

Word list

ich habe...verloren	I have lost
ikh hahba...fair lawren	
..meine Handschuhe..	my gloves
myna hunt shooa	
..meinen Hut..	my hat
mynen hoot	
..meinen Gürtel..	my belt
mynen girtle	
..meine Armbanduhr..	my watch
myna armbandoor	
..meine Strickjacke..	my cardigan
myna shtrik yukka	
..meine Brille..	my glasses
myna brilla	
..meinen Bleistift..	my pencil
mynen blyshtift	
..mein Etui..	my pencil case
mine aytoo ee	
..meine Filzstifte..	my felt tips
myna filts shtifta	
..mein Heft..	my exercise book
mine heft	
und	and
oont	

Du bist dran

Here is a German memory game that you can play with two or more players. One person starts by saying *ich habe* [ikh hahba], then the name of an object in German, then *verloren* [fair lawren]. You can use any of the objects on this page.

Take turns repeating what the person before has said but adding another object to the list each time. You only need to say *verloren* once, at the end of each turn. To say "and" in German, you say *und* [oont]. You are out if you can't remember everything in the right order or can't think of an object to add. The winner is the last one to be out.

Art class

Katja has painted a picture of an animal she particularly likes, using her favourite colour.

Look how she says which colour and animal she likes best.

Can you see which is Katja's painting?

Use the word list to help you match each of Katja's friends with their pictures.

Word list

mein Lieblingstier ist..	my favourite animal is..
mine leeblingsteer ist	
meine Lieblingsfarbe ist..	my favourite colour is..
myna leeblingsfarba ist	
die Katze	the cat
dee katsa	
der Hund	the dog
dair hoont	
das Kaninchen	the rabbit
dass ka neen khn	
die Maus	the mouse
dee mouse	
das Pferd	the horse
dass pfairt	
der Elefant	the elephant
dair ellayfunt	
das Schwein	the pig
dass shvine	

One animal on the word list isn't anyone's favourite. Can you spot which one it is?

Du bist dran
Tell someone in German which colour you like best. Try saying what your favourite animal is. You can use what Katja's friends are saying to help you.

Meine Lieblingsfarbe ist orange. Mein Lieblingstier ist das Pferd.

Meine Lieblingsfarbe ist gelb. Mein Lieblingstier ist das Kaninchen.

Meine Lieblingsfarbe ist braun. Mein Lieblingstier ist die Maus.

Colour guide

blau
blaow
rot
rawt
grün
grewn
orange
oronsh
gelb
gelp
lila
leelah
weiß
vice
schwarz
shvahrts
braun
brown

In German, colour words and other describing words (adjectives) often change their spelling and sound when they are used in different parts of sentences. On this page, they are all the same as on the guide.

Joke: Why are elephants big and grey?
If they were small and white, then they'd be snowflakes.

German calendar

Silvia and her friends are making German calendars which last for twelve years. You can make one too by following the instructions below.

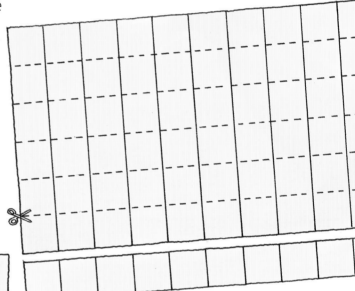

You will need:
2 sheets of cardboard about 29cm by 21cm (11in by 8in), scissors, pencils and felt tip pens, a ruler and some glue.

Use the word list to find out the names of the months in German. Look back at page 74 if you can't remember which day of the week is which.

1. Use the ruler to draw 3cm (1in) squares over one of the sheets of cardboard, then cut the sheet into strips lengthwise (each strip 3cm (1in) wide).

2. Each strip will have just over nine squares on it. On the first strip, leave one full blank square at either end, then write in the days of the week in German, one on each square, like this:

Sonntag	Montag	Dienstag	Mittwoch	Donnerstag	Freitag	Samstag

3. Stick the next two strips together to make one very long strip and mark numbers 1-16 on one side, again leaving a blank square at either end. Don't cut these off. Draw 3cm (1in) squares on the other side and write in numbers 17-31.

1	2	3	4	5	6	7	8	9	10	11	12	13	14	15	16

17	18	19	20	21	22	23	24	25	26	27	28	29	30	31

Word list

Januar *yan oo ar*	January	Juli *yoolie*	July	der Winter *dair vinter*	winter
Februar *fabe roo ar*	February	August *ow goost*	August	der Frühling *dair frewling*	spring
März *mairts*	March	September *zeptember*	September	der Sommer *dair zommer*	summer
April *apprill*	April	Oktober *oktawber*	October	der Herbst *dair hairpst*	autumm
Mai *my*	May	November *november*	November		
Juni *yoonie*	June	Dezember *day tsember*	December		

4. On the next strip write the months in German: *Januar* to *Juni* on one side and *Juli* to *Dezember* on the other. This time you will have more than one square left over. Don't cut them off as you will need them to pull the strips through the calendar.

5. The last strip is for the years. Write 1993 to 1998 on one side and 1999 to 2004 on the other.

6. Mark off the second sheet as shown below:

Cut slots along the lines. Thread your strips through to show the right day, date, month and year.

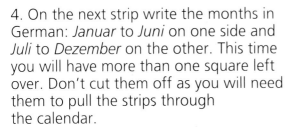

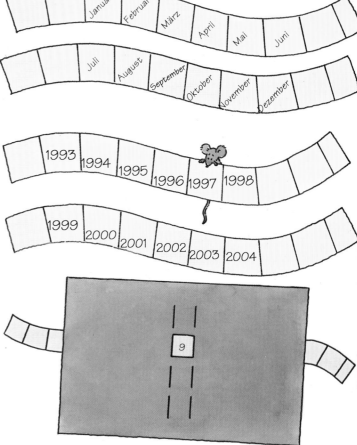

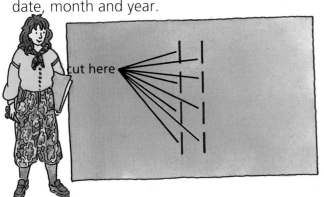

Silvia and the others are decorating an enormous calendar they have made for the classroom.

You could decorate the front of your calendar too, using the different seasons.

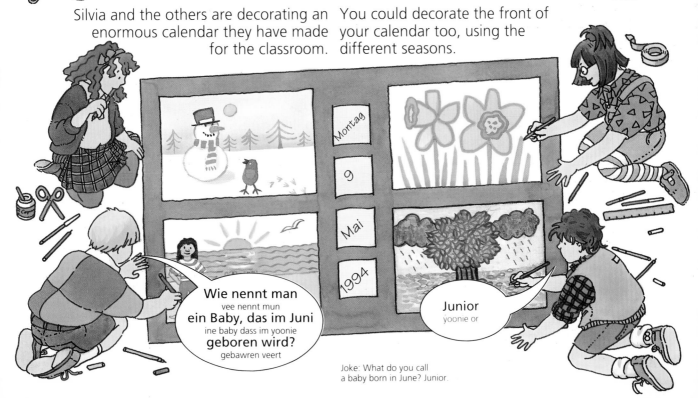

Joke: What do you call a baby born in June? Junior.

What is it?

Frau Ziffer has divided the class into teams to play a guessing game. The teams wear blindfolds and take turns to pick objects out of a large box. They must guess what they have picked out.

To ask what something is in German, you say *ist es...?* [ist ess], which means "is it...?" and then the name of the object.

To answer, you say *ja, es ist...* [yah ess ist], which means "yes, it's...", or *nein, es ist...* [nine ess ist], which means "no, it's...".

Using the word list to help you, can you answer everyone's questions?

Du bist dran
Point out to a friend something you know the name of in German and say *ist es...?* [ist ess] followed by a different name. Your friend must try and tell you the correct name, using *nein, es ist...* [nine ess ist].

Word list

ist es...? ist ess	is it...?	**ein Portemonnaie** ine port monnay	a purse
ja yah	yes	**ein Drachen** ine drakhen	a kite
nein nine	no	**eine Muschel** ine a mooshel	a shell
es ist ess ist	it is	**eine Pfeife** ine a pfyfa	a whistle
eine Blockflöte ine a blockflerta	a recorder	**ein Schläger** ine shlayger	a racket
ein Lutscher ine lootcher	a lollipop	**eine Armbanduhr** ine a armband oor	a wristwatch
ein Buch ine bookh	a book	**ein Bleistift** ine bly shtift	a pencil

82

Song

Here is a song to sing in German. Can you guess what any of the
words mean? You can check what they all mean on page 96.

Joke: What has eight legs, two wheels and goes fast?
A spider on a motorbike.

83

Hide and seek

Katja and Markus are playing hide and seek. It's Markus's turn to hide. Can you spot him? (If you can't remember who Markus is, look back to page 69.)

To say, "There he is," in German you say *Da ist er* [dah ist air].

Wo ist Katja? [vaw ist katya]. Where is Katja? To say, "There she is," you say *Da ist sie* [dah ist zee].

Which paths must Katja take to reach Markus by the shortest route? She cannot use any of the paths which are blocked by children or objects.

Word list

wo ist	where is
vaw ist	
da ist er	there he, it is
dah ist air	
da ist sie	there she, it is
dah ist zee	
da ist es	there it is
dah ist ess	
die Katze	cat
dee katsa	
das Fahrrad	bicycle
dass fahrraht	
der Drachen	kite
dair drukhen	
die Fahne	flag
dee fahna	
der Gärtner	gardener
dair gairtner	

Can you spot some other things in the picture? Say *Da ist er* [dah ist air] when you spot a *der* word, *Da ist sie* [dah ist zee] for a *die* word and *Da ist es* [dah ist ess] for a *das* word.

Wo ist der Drachen?

Wo ist die Katze?

Wo ist das Fahrrad?

84 Wo ist die Fahne?

Joke: What goes clip-clop, clip thud?
A horse with a wooden leg.

Tongue twister

How fast can you say this tongue twister without making any mistakes?

Fischers Fritz fischt
fishers frits fisht
frische Fische. Frische Fische
frisha fisha frisha fisha
fischt Fischers Fritz.
fisht fishers frits

85

Here is what it means in English: *The Fischers' Fritz fishes fresh fish. Fresh fish is what the Fischers' Fritz fishes.*

Sports day

Today is sports day. Frau Ziffer is asking who knows how to climb, *Wer kann klettern?* [vair kan klettern]. Silvia answers, *Ich kann klettern* [ikh kan klettern] which means, "I know how to climb".

Use the word list to help you answer these questions for the people in the picture. Point to someone who is doing each activity and say *ich kann* [ikh kan] for them and then what he or she is doing.

Wer kann Handstand machen?
Wer kann laufen?
Wer kann kriechen?
Wer kann einen Purzelbaum machen?
Wer kann ein Rad schlagen?
Wer kann hüpfen?
Wer kann springen?

Joke: Doctor, the invisible man's waiting for you.
Tell him I can't see him.

86

Word list

wer kann...? *vair kan*	who can...?	**einen Purzelbaum machen** *ine n poortselbaowm makhen*	to do a somersault
ich kann *ikh kan*	I can	**hüpfen** *hoopfen*	to hop
kannst du...? *kanst doo*	can you...?	**kriechen** *kreekhen*	to crawl
laufen *laowfen*	to run	**klettern** *klettern*	to climb
Handstand machen *huntshtunt makhen*	to do a handstand	**springen** *shpringen*	to jump
ein Rad schlagen *ine raht shlahgn*	to do a cartwheel		

German flip-flaps

Here is how to make and use a German flip-flap.

You will need:

a large square of paper and some felt tips.

Fold each corner of your paper square into the middle. Turn the paper over and do the same on the other side.

Write numbers 2 to 9, one on each of the small triangles you can now see.

Lift up the four flaps in turn. Under each number, write down *kannst du* [kanst doo], which means "can you" followed by one of the activites from the word list. You will have to write in little writing to fit in all the words.

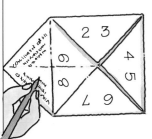

Fold the flaps in again and turn the square back over.

Write *blau, rot, grün* and *gelb* on the four small squares. Fill them in with your felt tips. (Look back at page 78 if you can't remember which ones to use).

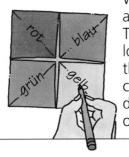

Slide both your index fingers and thumbs under the squares and push them together like this:

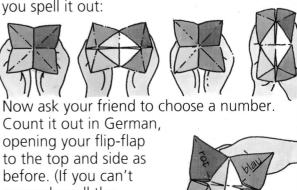

Ask a friend to choose a square. Say the word on it, then do this as you spell it out:

Now ask your friend to choose a number. Count it out in German, opening your flip-flap to the top and side as before. (If you can't remember all the numbers in German, look back at page 72.)

When you finish counting, ask your friend to choose another number. This time, open up that flap and read out loud in German what it says under the number your friend has chosen. Your friend must do the activity you read, or start again.

87

Lunchtime

Today, lunch is outside. Unfortunately, not everyone seems to be having a good time.

Birgit [beer git] is in a bad mood because she has ripped her skirt. *Ich bin schlecht gelaunt* [ikh bin shlekht gelaownt] means, "I am in a bad mood," in German.

How do you think the other children are feeling? Use the word list to help you match each speech bubble below with a child in the picture. Can you say each one out loud in German?

Mir ist heiß.

Mir ist kalt.

Ich habe Hunger.

Ich habe Durst.

Ich habe Durst.

Ich habe Hunger.

Ich bin glücklich.

Ich bin müde.

Ich bin traurig.

Ich habe Hunger.

Du bist dran

How do you feel at the moment?

Use the word list to describe how you feel in German. Say it out loud.

Ich bin schlecht gelaunt.

Nenne mir
nenna meer
dreißig Tiere, die
dryssikh teera dee
aus Afrika kommen.
owss afree kah kommen

Neunundzwanzig
noyn oont tsvantsikh
Elefanten und eine
ellayfunten oont ine a
Giraffe.
gear affa

Joke: Name 30 animals which come from Africa.
29 elephants and a giraffe.

Word list

In German, describing words (adjectives) often change their sound and spelling. This depends on whether they describe *der* words (masculine), *die* words (feminine) or *das* words (neuter) and where they come in a sentence. On this page, all the adjectives stay the same.

ich habe Hunger ikh hahba hoonger	I'm hungry
ich habe Durst ikh hahba doorst	I'm thirsty
mir ist heiß meer ist hyss	I'm hot
mir ist kalt meer ist kalt	I'm cold
ich bin ikh bin	I am
glücklich glooklikh	happy
traurig traowrikh	sad
müde mooda	tired
schlecht gelaunt shlekht gelaownt	in a bad mood

Telling the time

Karin must meet Silvia and Katja from school today but her watch is broken so she has to keep asking the time.

To ask the time in German, you say *Wie spät ist es?* [vee shpate ist ess]. To answer, you say *es ist* [ess ist] which means "it is" and then the time.

Uhr [oor] after a number on the clock means "o'clock".

So to say, "It's ten o'clock," in German, you say *Es ist zehn Uhr* [ess ist tsain oor]. How do you say, "It's six o'clock"?

Can you say *Es ist... Uhr* for each of the hours on Oma Strudel's alarm clock?

Now can you spot what time it is in each of these pictures? Answer Karin's question in each one by saying the time out loud in German. Use Oma Strudel's alarm clock to help you with the numbers.

Word list

wie spät ist es? what time is it?
vee shpate ist ess
es ist ... Uhr it's...o'clock
ess ist ...oor
Mittag midday
mittahg
Mitternacht midnight
mitternahkht
halb...* half ...
hulp

*In German, instead of saying "half past", you say "half to" the next hour. So to say "half past one", you say *es ist halb zwei* [ess ist hulp tsvy].

90   A

You don't say *halb* with *Mitternacht* or *Mittag*. You say *halb zwölf* [hulp tsverlf].

"One o'clock" is *ein Uhr*, but "one" on its own is *eins* [ine ts]. To say "half past twelve", you say *halb eins* [hulp ine ts].

zwölf Uhr
tsverlf oor

elf Uhr
elf oor

zehn Uhr
tsain oor

neun Uhr
noynoor

acht Uhr
akht oor

sieben Uhr
zeebn oor

ein Uhr
ine oor

zwei Uhr
tsvy oor

drei Uhr
dry oor

vier Uhr
feer oor

fünf Uhr
foonf oor

sechs Uhr
zex oor

Es ist acht Uhr.

Wie spät ist es?

B

Wie spät ist es?

Wie spät ist es?

E

C

Wie spät ist es?

D

Wie spät ist es?

Du bist dran

Wie spät ist es? [vee shpate ist ess].
Can you say in German what time it is
at the moment? Say it to the nearest
half hour. In German, you say "half to"
the next hour instead of "half-past". So
if you want to say "half-past" you say
halb [hulp] and then the hour after the
one you mean. To say "half past four",
you would say *halb fünf* [hulp foonf].

Es
ist fünf
Uhr.

Es ist halb
zwölf.

91

True or false?

Katja and Silvia are playing a game on the way home from school. One of them says something and the other has to say whether it is true or false.

To say, "That's true," in German, say *Das ist richtig* [dass ist rikhtikh]. To say, "That's false," say *Das ist falsch* [dass ist fulsh].

Can you say what the reply to each of their speech bubbles should be? Say the answers out loud. If you don't know, say *Ich weiß es nicht* [ikh vice ess nikht] which means, "I don't know".

Look back through the book if you can't remember any of the words.

Word list

das ist richtig — that's true
dass ist rikhtikh

das ist falsch — that's false
dass ist fulsh

ich weiß es nicht — I don't know
ikh vice ess nikht

das ist — this/that is
dass ist

What's the right word?

Frau Ziffer stays late at school to correct everyone's work. Can you help her? Say out loud in German what should be written under each picture.

Das ist [dass ist] means "this is" or "that is". Look back through this part of the book if you can't remember any of the words you need.

Mein Buch ist blau.

Es gibt drei Drachen.

Mein Bruder heißt Oma Strudel.

Du bist dran

You could make your own picture book in German. Draw something and write what it is in German, using *das ist* [dass ist] and then the name of the object. Remember to check if it is a *der*, *die* or *das* object, so that you know to write *ein* (for *der* and *das* words) or *eine* (for *die* words) before it.

93

Word list (part 3)

Here is a list of all the German words and phrases** used in this part of the book in alphabetical order. You can use the list either to check quickly what a word means or to test yourself. Cover up any German or English word or phrase and see if you can say its translation. Remember that most words change slightly when you are talking about more than one thing (plural).

German	Pronunciation	English
acht	akht	*eight*
achtzehn	akht tsain	*eighteen*
April	apprill	*April*
Arm (der)	arm	*arm*
Armbanduhr (die)	armbandoor	*watch*
August	ow goost*	*August*
Bein (das)	bine	*leg*
blau	blaow	*blue*
Bleistift (der),	blyshtift	*pencil*
Bleistifte (die)	blyshtifta	*pencils*
Blockflöte (die)	blokflerta	*recorder*
braun	brown	*brown*
Brille (die)	brilla	*glasses*
Bruder (der)	brooder	*brother*
Buch (das),	bookh	*book*
Bücher (die)	boosher	*books*
da ist er	dah ist air	*there he, it is*
da ist es	dah ist es	*there it is*
da ist sie	dah ist zee	*there she, it is*
danke	dunka	*thank you*
das ist	dass ist	*this is, that is*
der, die, das	dair, dee, dass	*the*
Deutsch	doytch	*German*
Dezember	day tsember	*December*
Dienstag (der)	deenstahg	*Tuesday*
Donnerstag (der)	donnerstahg	*Thursday*
Drachen (der)	drakhen	*kite*
drei	dry	*three*
dreizehn	dry tsain	*thirteen*
du bist dran	doo bist dran	*your turn*
ein, eine	ine, ine a	*one, a*
ein Rad schlagen	ine raht shlahgn	*to do a cartwheel*
einen Purzelbaum machen	inen poortselbaowm makhen	*to do a somersault*
eins	ine ts	*one*
Elefant (der)	ellayfunt	*elephant*
elf	elf	*eleven*
Englisch	eng glish	*English*
Entschuldigung	entshooldigoong	*sorry*
er heißt	air hyste	*he is called*
(es geht mir) sehr gut	ess gate meer zair goot	*I'm very well*
es gibt	ess gipt	*there is, there are*
es ist	ess ist	*it is*
es ist ... Uhr	ess ist oor	*it is ... o'clock*
Etui (das)	aytoo ee	*pencil case*
Fahne (die)	fahna	*flag*
Fahrrad (das)	fahrraht	*bicycle*
falsch	fulsh	*false*
Februar	fabe roo ar	*February*
Filzstift (der),	filts shtift	*felt tip pen*
Filzstifte (die)	filts shtifta	*felt tip pens*
Frau (die)	fraow	*Mrs. , woman*
Freitag (der)	frytahg	*Friday*
Frühling (der)	frewling	*spring*
fünf	foonf*	*five*
fünfzehn	foonf* tsain	*fifteen*
fuß	fooss	*foot*
Gärtner (der)	gairtner	*gardener*
gelb	gelp	*yellow*
Geschenk (das),	geshenk	*present*
Geschenke (die)	geshenka	*presents*
glücklich	glooklikh*	*happy*
grün	grewn	*green*
Gürtel (der)	girtle	*belt*
Guten Tag	gootn tahg	*hello*
halb	hulp	*half*
Hallo	hullaw	*hi*
Hand (die)	hunt (dee)	*hand*
Handschuh (der),	hunt shoo	*glove*
Handschuhe (die)	hunt shooa	*gloves*
Handstand machen	huntshtunt makhen	*to do a handstand*
Heft (das)	heft	*exercise book*
Herbst (der)	hairpst	*autumn*
Herr	hair	*Mr.*
heute	hoyta	*today*
Himmel-und-Hölle	himmel oont* herla	*hopscotch*
Hund (der)	hoont*	*dog*
hüpfen	hoopfen*	*to hop*
Hut (der),	hoot,	*hat,*
Hüte (die)	hoota	*hats*
ich bin	ikh bin	*I am*
ich habe ... verloren	ikh hahba fairlawren	*I have lost*
ich habe Bauchweh	ikh hahba baowkhvay	*I have a tummy-ache*
ich habe Durst	ikh hahba doorst	*I'm thirsty*

94

*The "oo" sound in these words is like the "u" in "put".
**Except those in the jokes and songs, which are translated on the pages or on the answer page.

German	Pronunciation	English
ich habe Hunger	ikh hahba hoonger*	I'm hungry
ich habe Kopfweh	ikh hahba kopfvay	I have a headache
ich habe Zahnweh	ikh hahba tsahnvay	I have toothache
ich heiße	ikh hyssa	I am called
ich kann	ikh kan	I can
ich weiß es nicht	ikh vice ess nikht	I don't know
ist es...?	ist ess...?	is it...?
ja	yah	yes
Januar	yan oo ar	January
Juli	yoolie	July
Juni	yoonie	June
kannst du ...?	kanst doo	can you...?
Katze (die)	katsa	cat
klettern	klettern	to climb
kriechen	kreekhen	to crawl
laufen	laowfen	to run
lila	leelah	purple
Lutscher (der)	lootcher*	lollipop
Mai	my	May
März	mairts	March
Maus (die)	mouse	mouse
mein Bein tut mir weh	mine bine toot meer vay	my leg hurts
mein Lieblingstier ist...	mine leeblingsteer ist	my favourite animal is...
mein, meine, meinen	mine, myna, mynen	my
meine Lieblingsfarbe ist...	myna leeblingsfarba ist	my favourite colour is...
mir ist heiß	meer ist hyss	I'm hot
mir ist kalt	meer ist kalt	I'm cold
Mittag	mittahg	midday
Mitternacht	mitternahkht	midnight
Mittwoch (der)	mitvokh	Wednesday
Montag (der)	mawntahg	Monday
müde	mooda	tired
Muschel (die)	mooshel*	shell
Musik	moozeek	music
Mutter (die)	mootter*	mother
nein	nine	no
neun	noyn	nine
neunzehn	noyn tsain	nineteen
November	november	November
Oktober	oktawber	October
Oma (die)	awma	Granny
Onkel (der)	onkel	uncle
orange	oronsh	orange
Pfeife (die)	pfyffa	whistle
Pferd (das)	pfairt	horse
Pflanze (die), Pflanzen (die)	pfluntsa pfluntsen	plant plants
Portemonnaie (das)	port monnay	purse
Regenschirm (der), Regenschirme (die)	raygn sheerm raygn sheerma	umbrella umbrellas
richtig	rikhtikh	true
rot	rawt	red
Samstag (der)	zamstahg	Saturday
Schläger (der)	shlayger	racket
schlecht gelaunt	shlekht gelaownt	in a bad mood
schwarz	shvahrts	black
Schwein (das)	shvine	pig
Schwester (die)	shvester	sister
sechs	zex	six
sechzehn	zekh tsain	sixteen
September	zeptember	September
sie heißt	zee hyste	she is called
sieben	zeebn	seven
siebzehn	zeep tsain	seventeen
Sommer (der)	zommer	summer
Sonntag (der)	zonntahg	Sunday
Sport	shport	sport
springen	shpringen	to jump
Strickjacke (die)	shtrik yukka	cardigan
traurig	traowrikh	sad
und	oont*	and
Vater (der)	fahter	father
vier	feer	four
vierzehn	feer tsain	fourteen
weiß	vice	white
wer kann ... ?	vair kan	who can...?
wie geht's?	vee gates	how are you?
wie heißt du?	vee hyste doo	what's your name?
wie spät ist es?	vee shpate ist ess	what's the time?
Winter (der)	vinter	winter
wo ist...?	vaw ist	where is...?
Wochenende (das)	vokhen enda	week-end
zehn	tsain	ten
Zeichnen	tsykhnen	drawing, art
zwanzig	tsvan tsikh	twenty
zwei	tsvy	two
zwölf	tsverlf	twelve

Answers (part 3)

PAGE 68-69

This is the way Jörg should go:

Here are the German answers to the questions:
Sie heißt Silvia.
Er heißt Herr Strudel.

PAGE 70-71

Frau Strudel should say, *Mein Bein tut mir weh.*
Oma Strudel should say, *Es geht mir sehr gut.*
Herr Strudel should say, *Ich habe Kopfweh.*
Rainer should say, *Ich habe Bauchweh.*

PAGE 72-73

Es gibt acht Pflanzen.   *Es gibt neun Bleistifte.*
Es gibt drei   *Es gibt sieben Hüte.*
  Regenschirme.   *Es gibt fünf Geschenke.*

Here is the tune for the song:

1. Ein Hund woll - te spiel'n, woll - te Fuß - ball spiel - en,
   ine hoont voll ta shpeeln voll ta fooss bal shpeel en

   Ein Hund und sein Herr woll - ten Fuß - ball spiel - en.
   ine hoont oont zine hair voll ten fooss bal shpeel en

2. Zwei Hund' woll - ten spiel'n, woll - ten Fuß - ball spiel - en,
   tsvy hoont voll ten shpeeln voll ten fooss bal shpeel en

   Zwei Hund', ein Hund und sein Herr woll - ten Fuß - ball spiel-en.
   tsvy hoont ine hoont oont zine hair voll ten fooss bal shpeel en

3. Drei Hund' woll - ten spiel'n, woll - ten Fuß - ball spiel - en,
   dry hoont voll ten shpeeln voll ten fooss bal shpeel en

   Drei Hund', zwei Hund', ein Hund und sein Herr woll-ten Fuß-ball spiel-en.
   dry hoont tsvy hoont ine hoont oont zine hair voll ten fooss bal shpeel en

PAGE 74-75

A. *Es ist Montag.*   C. *Es ist Freitag.*
B. *Es ist Donnerstag.*   D. *Es ist Dienstag.*

PAGE 78-79

Der Elefant (the elephant) isn't anyone's favourite.

PAGE 82-83

This is what the words mean in English:
What is that there? What do I see?
It is really heavenly.
It is not a mad pig,
Nor can it be a snake,
What is that there? What do I see?
My cat. She loves me.

PAGE 84-85

This is the way Katja should go:

PAGE 90-91

A. *Es ist neun Uhr.*   D. *Es ist drei Uhr.*
B. *Es ist elf Uhr.*   E. *Es ist vier Uhr.*
C. *Es ist ein Uhr.*

PAGE 92-93

A. *Das ist falsch.*   D. *Das ist richtig.*
B. *Das ist richtig.*   E. *Das ist falsch.*
C. *Das ist falsch.*   F. *Das ist falsch.*

Here is what should be written under each picture:
A. *Das ist ein Hund.*   D. *Das ist ein Bleistift.*
B. *Das ist ein Buch.*   E. *Das ist mein Vater.*
C. *Das ist ein Hut.*